D1588218

The Ring in the
Rough Stuff

25p·

by the same author

THE AFFAIR OF
THE ROCKERBYE BABY

THE GHOSTS
(filmed as *The Amazing Mr Blunden*)

ANTONIA BARBER

The Ring in the Rough Stuff

JONATHAN CAPE
THIRTY BEDFORD SQUARE LONDON

First published 1983
Copyright © 1983 by Barbara Anthony
Jonathan Cape Ltd, 30 Bedford Square, London WC1

British Library Cataloguing in Publication Data

Barber, Antonia
The ring in the rough stuff.
I. Title
823'.914[J] PZ7

ISBN 0-224-02076-5

Printed and bound in Great Britain by
Mackays of Chatham Ltd

To my own Jo, Nick and Gem,
who wanted a story with a bit of rough stuff

Author's Note

In a remote mud hole on the Medway saltings, the rotting hulk of an old sailing barge and the rusting hull of a First World War submarine lie side by side. For most of the year they rest in peaceful obscurity beneath the wide, forgiving waters of the estuary, but any reader who cares to go in search may find them at low-water springs. A number of suggestions, most of them very dull, have been put forward to explain how the two wrecks come to be there; but since neither can be positively identified, no one will ever know for sure. This story gives another possible explanation, and though I cannot prove that it is the correct one, it is just as likely as the others and much more fun.

The history of the Medway brick fields and of the Thames sailing barges is rich in humorous stories and I have tried to include them in my book wherever possible. I am therefore indebted to all those who have collected and written down these tales, especially Frank G.

Willmott, whose book *Bricks and 'Brickies'* (published privately, 1972) is a mine of useful information. Readers who wish to know more about the sailing barges may also like to read Captain Jim Uglow's classic, *Sailorman* (Conway Maritime Press, Greenwich, 1975). Punchy Kitson's account of his barge race is based on a tale I once heard told by a great barge Skipper, Mr Jimmy Diddams.

Finally, may I thank Alan Reekie and Rhondda of the sailing barge *Ironsides* for their encouragement and help with the manuscript of this book, and for first sharing with me their own enthusiasm for the world of the Thames sailing barges.

A.B.

One

There were rats in the rough stuff.

It came down by barge from the Thames-side wharves of Vauxhall and Blackfriars, Battersea and Chelsea, and you could see from the shore the swarms of flies that hovered about it and crawled in vast numbers over the stinking heaps. It came from the refuse bins of London and the barge crews hated it, not only for the stench and the ever-present flies, but because the "London mixture" was full of coke cinders from the coal fires of the city. These gave off a heavy vapour which seeped down into the crews' quarters, until they were hard put to choose between the flies up on deck and the fumes down below.

But there was no escaping it, for the refuse they brought down to the brickworks was an essential ingredient of the bricks they carried on the journey up river, and the expanding city rose like a phoenix from the burned ashes of her own refuse.

When the rough stuff reached the Lower Field

Brickyard, it was unloaded into carts, dumped in vast, mouldering piles and left until the fish heads and the cabbage stalks, the old bones and the turnip tops, had rotted away or been consumed by the hordes of rats which soon set up home in it. What remained a year or so later were big lumps of coke, which meant cheap fuel for the brick kilns, and small cinders and ash, which could be mixed with the clay as the bricks were made to fuse with the pug during the firing. To separate the one from the other, and to pick out any old boots, broken china and rusting metal that had survived the ravages of the rats, the Lower Field Brickworks employed a gang of boys, each of whom was duly rewarded at the end of a hard week's sifting and scavenging with the princely sum of half a crown.

On the whole, the boys had no complaints. Their fathers and their grandfathers had started in the same way, and had gone on to become brick moulders, crowders and sorters sometimes making as much as forty pounds in a good season. Employment in the brick field was a family affair. Now that their fathers had gone to the war, even their mothers sometimes worked alongside the older men, loading the bricks into the barrows and helping out with the lighter jobs.

The boys who sorted the rough stuff had a natural affinity for dirt that enabled them to relish a task which their elders would have found more distasteful. They were used to the flies; they waged war on rats; and they passed their leisure moments making intricate traps to catch the plump starlings which came to plunder the riches of the rough stuff and frequently ended up in home-made pies.

And as if these were not delights enough, there was always the outside chance that some day some prize would turn up as they sieved through the heaps: a sovereign swept up unseen in a dark corner in a house in Vauxhall; a small silver spoon left in the bottom of the sink by a careless skivvy in Battersea and later thrown out with the potato peelings; or even some valuable trinket from a smart house in Chelsea. It was not that these finds were frequent: on the contrary, it was rare for them to find anything more valuable than a threepenny piece. But the ever-present possibility was like owning a ticket in the Irish Sweepstake: however long the odds might be, it still added an extra dimension of excitement to their lives.

With all these advantages, it was really most unreasonable of Daniel Swann not to like his job. He had been glad enough to get it. With his father fighting somewhere in France and his mother in poor health, the money he brought home made the difference between survival and a swift descent into debt and disaster. For this reason old Mr Jarvis, the manager of the Lower Field, who was a strict but not unkindly man, had turned a blind eye to the fact that he was barely twelve and by rights should still have been in school. Daniel ought to have been deeply grateful to Mr Jarvis, and he was; he should therefore have worked with a will, however unsavoury the task, but alas he did not. For one thing, he hated the rats: their small red eyes glistened in the depths of their dark holes; they had sharp teeth to bite the probing hand which encountered them unexpectedly; they moved in a sudden, unpredictable scurry, which always took him by surprise so that he jumped back and the older boys laughed at him.

"Look out, Danny!" they cried. "Or a big 'un 'ull drag

you down 'is 'ole!"

"Swallow 'im in a gulp I reckon! You wanna watch out young Danny!"

He did not even enjoy it much when the boys passed their dinner break in getting their own back on the rats. Each clutching a large hunk of bread in one unwashed hand and a heavy stick in the other, they pranced and hollered while their small fierce terriers drove the enemy out from the reeking piles. Then, "Thwack!" Down came their weapons with the accuracy of long practice, and the squealing fugitives were reduced to a flattened mess of blood and fur. It made Daniel feel sick. He tried hard not to show it, for it seemed an unmanly reaction when the others all enjoyed it so much, but there were days when he found it hard to get his lunch down.

He felt even worse when they caught the birds. He knew well enough that it was stupid to eat chickens which he had fed by hand, or pigeons which his father had often shot in the old days, and then feel squeamish about starlings. But when he arrived early in the morning and saw them beating their wings in frenzy against the bars of the make-shift bird traps, he had more than once been moved to set them free, and dreaded the day when the older boys would catch him doing it. Once when they had made a particularly good haul, they had offered him half a dozen of the small, limp, black bodies tied up with a piece of string, and he had not liked to refuse. It was a generous gesture: food was short at home and although they were fiddly to prepare, they were said to be as delicious as the quails which were eaten at rich men's tables. But his mother had wept over the small feathered corpses and his sister Rosie, who was seven, had beaten him with small, angry fists and refused to speak to him for three days, even though he had pleaded that he had taken no part in the original slaughter.

But it was not the fear of the rats, or the unsavoury work, or even the feeling that he did not fit in with the older boys, which prevented him from putting his heart into his work. The truth was that Daniel's heart had been given away, when he was barely old enough to walk, to the sturdy, heavy-laden, Thames barges with their great tan sails, which passed in an unending procession up and down the river. Beautiful, industrious, sailing work-horses, they carried bricks and cement, mud and rough stuff, along the Thames and the Medway, and a hundred other freights which were unloaded into them from the big ships in the London docks and delivered all along the south and east coasts of England.

When he was a baby he had clapped his hands with excitement as they approached the shore where his mother stood holding him, and when a change of tack took them away across the river, he had kicked and screamed his disapproval till the next one came along. When he was old enough to walk, his father had made him a rough little model with sails cut from an old brown skirt of his mother's, and had taken him to sail it in the sandy pools of the foreshore when the tide was low. As he grew older he built his own models, each one larger and more detailed than the last, until suddenly there was no more joy to be had from models and toys, and he knew that he had reached the age when nothing but the real thing would satisfy him. Unfortunately, a twelve-year-old, not particularly large for his age, was not considered old enough for even the most menial tasks on board. So he was obliged to spend his days sorting out the rough stuff, which was particularly hard because it meant working with his back to the river. Whenever the pull was too strong and he turned his head to watch the sails go past, the older boys would shout; "Skivin' agin' then, Danny! 'Ere comes old Jarvis after you!" Or if they were in more humorous mood, "Look out, young Danny! There's a rat just gorn up yer trouser leg!" And when, his mind being elsewhere, he fell for this ploy, they would fall around laughing and shouting, "Cor, that Danny, 'e ain't 'alf a card!"

And so his life might have gone on indefinitely — or at least until old Mr Jarvis found him slacking once too often, and instead of his usual stern admonition to "Stop day-dreaming lad, and put your back into the job!" finally gave him the sack — if Daniel had not found the ring in the rough stuff.

He first saw it as a sudden red gleam in the depths of a dark hole and, ever wary of the rats, he hastily drew back his hand, dislodging the gleam as he did so. For a moment he thought he saw the sunlight catch gold, and then it fell down and down through numberless black caverns between the decaying cinders and was lost from sight. His immediate thought was to call to the other boys and take the pile apart in search of the treasure. But he was not a boy who acted upon impulse and more cautious second thoughts came hard upon the first. He had not actually seen anything, and if he made a great hullabaloo and there was nothing there the boys would tease him and say he was dreaming again. His third thought was even more practical. Everyone, even Mr Jarvis himself, respected the time-honoured rule of "finders keepers" where the treasures of the rough stuff were concerned: but did an uncertain glimpse of he knew not what actually amount to finding something? Or would the trinket, if trinket there were, belong to the lad who actually laid hands on it? He decided that he could not take the risk: if there was something there, he must find it himself.

And so, for the next few days, he worked through his pile with a rare degree of concentration, so that the boys scratched their heads and said, "Reckon 'e's sickening for something!" and old Mr Jarvis, who missed nothing that went on in the Lower Field, nodded his head sagely and told himself that Swann's lad was finally settling down into a good steady worker like his father. Daniel sieved and sorted his way right down to ground level, and had just made up his mind that he had imagined the whole thing, when suddenly he saw it again: a gold ring with a red stone. It was lodged between a large lump of coke and a rusty door handle, and for a moment he just stared, unable to believe his good fortune. It was nothing very elaborate, just a thin band of gold set with a simple red stone, but it was the satisfaction of having tracked it down, of knowing that he had not been mistaken, that filled him with a sense of triumph.

If he had come across it unexpectedly, he would have cried out in his excitement, bringing the other boys crowding round; but coming upon it at the end of a long search, he simply stared at it without even picking it up. Should he pretend to have found it by chance? He felt that his cries of astonishment would lack conviction. Should he confess that he had been hunting it for days? Then the other boys would think him mean not to have let them in on the excitement. Perhaps he had been mean . . . as he was wrestling with a sudden sense of guilt, he was startled by a voice close behind him:

"Now I know you're up to summat, young Danny!"

Daniel jumped nervously and with a swift, instinctive movement gathered up the ring and concealed it in his hand; but the voice went on, "It's one thing to give up boat watching and get on with yer job, but to work on through yer dinner break, well, that don't look good!"

"Oi reckon he's planning to be gaffer," put in a second voice, "and lord it over us all. Ain't that right, young 'un?"

"Yes," said Daniel nervously, "I mean, no . . . I didn't hear the hooter."

"Ah! 'Tis all right then," the boy sounded reassured. "The lad's just back to his day-dreaming agin. Well, wake up, our Danny, 'cos Tom and Josh 'ave gone for their dogs and we're gonna 'ave a rat bashin'!"

Daniel slid his hand unobtrusively into his trouser pocket and realized that it was the one with the hole in it. He looked around hastily for some escape, both to avoid the "rat bashin' " and to transfer the ring to his good pocket without revealing it. It no longer seemed possible to share the news of his find with the others without drawing attention to his initial secretiveness.

Down at the quayside, his searching eyes spotted a barge coming alongside. He recognized her trim paint-work at once and the tall, curly-haired figure standing in her bows with the mooring line. His face lit up and he waved joyfully.

"It's Jem and the *Windhawk*," he said. "Sorry Billy, sorry Jack, I'll see you all later," and grabbing his dinner tin he ran down to the quayside in time to catch the line as it was thrown ashore. As he went, he passed the ring into his other hand and, hardly conscious of what he did, stuffed it carelessly into his good pocket, where it joined company with three marbles, a hop-scotch stone, a thin piece of rope with a half-finished splice in the end, a decidedly grubby handkerchief, and a large gob-stopper, only slightly sucked, which Rosie had thrust into his hand as he left the house that morning.

Two

Sitting on the *Windhawk's* hatch-covers, eating his bread
and cheese, and sipping a big mug of tea which Jem had
brewed up on the little iron stove below, Daniel was in
another world. It felt different: the constant, almost
imperceptible motion of the heavy barge alongside,
settling herself comfortably into the mud of her berth as
the tide dropped, a sense that the boards beneath his feet
were somehow alive. It smelt different too: no longer the
sweet–sour decaying stink of the rough stuff, but a sharp
clean smell, which made him think of crabs and long green
banners of weed and a day at the seaside.

"What you got on then?" he asked, breathing in deeply
and letting the sharp, salt tang of it scour the last trace of
the refuse heaps from his lungs. The outward breath was
like a deep sigh of contentment.

"Load of Leigh sand. Took a freight of bricks up the
Blackwater to Maldon: old Jarvis said put into Southend
on the way back for a load of sand. *Kappa's* on the blocks

for a repaint and they were getting a bit low."

Daniel nodded, his mouth full of bread and sweet tea. He wished desperately that he were eight years older and a barge mate like Jem. He glanced across at the object of his envy: tall and handsome, with a sun-brown face under dark curling hair, Jem sat gazing morosely down at the deck planks while his tea grew cold and a thin brown skin settled unbroken on the surface.

"Drink yer tea," said Daniel.

Jem grunted but made no move; he was moping again. Daniel couldn't understand it: Jem had everything in life that he would have given his eye teeth for, and all he wanted to do was to chuck it up and go to fight in the war. He didn't have to go, he was doing a valuable job, but only his father's threats and his mother's pleas kept him from volunteering. His father, "Punchy" Kitson (nicknamed for his love of a fight and a powerful "left" in his youth), planned to retire as soon as the war was over. Not that he had reached retirement age, but he had had the wit and extreme good fortune many years before to marry the Adorable Dora, only daughter of old Jim Midgeley, a retired ganger who had made his money in the clay digging and had bought the Anchor and Hope, the ale-house by the Lower Field. Jim's wife had died when Dora was born, and perhaps he had spoiled his daughter a little. Certainly by the time she was eighteen she was not only a fine figure of a woman with a pair of eyes famed along the length of the river, she was also strong minded and independent, and invariably did just as she pleased. So it was that throughout her marriage to Punchy and the raising of her son Jem she had continued to reign supreme behind her father's bar, and after his death a few years earlier she had taken over the licence herself and now ran the old pub in her own right.

Since twenty-two years of marriage and motherhood had done nothing to diminish her ample charm, or to lessen the admiration of all the brickies, muddies, and sailormen who frequented her bar, Punchy had begun to see the advantages of an early retirement from the barges to help run the pub and keep an eye on her. Indeed he had only stayed on as Skipper of the *Windhawk* until Jem should be old and experienced enough to step into his shoes. So his reaction to Jem's sudden urge to run away to war, leaving the barge to pass into other hands, had been crisp, to the point and quite unprintable. Daniel's sympathies were entirely with Punchy for he had his own plan, which was that, when Jem took over as Skipper, he himself would take Jem's place as mate. He had not mentioned this scheme to anyone for fear that they would not take him seriously, but he saw that if Jem abandoned the *Windhawk* now, and Punchy took on a new mate, things would never be the same.

"What yer want to go and fight for anyway?" he demanded suddenly, unable to endure the long silence.

But instead of the usual impassioned speech about King and Country (all of which Jem had mugged up from recruitment posters, since the truth was that he thought going to war would be more exciting than sailing the *Windhawk* up and down the Thames) Jem continued to stare gloomily at his feet.

Daniel tried again. "Jem! What yer want to go and fight for?"

The cries of the boys and the barking of dogs and the thwacking of sticks reached his ears distantly from the direction of the rough stuff. He had a sudden mental picture of war with men instead of rats, scattered across the ground, spilling their blood and guts into the wet mud. He thought of his own father, fighting in the thick of it, and he shuddered.

"I reckon only a fool would go to war if he didn't have to!"

"Oh, that," said Jem without interest. "No, I changed my mind . . . I don't want to go after all." But he still looked as dismal as ever.

"What's the matter then?" Daniel could hardly believe his ears at this sudden about-face, nor could he see what else Jem could be pining about. His half-hour dinner break would soon be over and he searched about for some way of getting Jem's attention. Then he remembered and stuffed his hand into his pocket.

"Here, Jem!" he said. "You know that splice you were showing me? Well, I've got in a bit of a muddle."

He tugged at the piece of rope and out came the grubby handkerchief too; the marbles and the gob-stopper rattled across the deck and the ring fell glinting seductively right at Jem's feet.

They both stared at it in silence for a long time: then Jem reached out one foot and turned the ring around with the toe of his heavy boot. He frowned thoughtfully, then bent down, picked it up, and looked at it carefully from all angles.

"Where did yer get that then?" he asked.

"Found it in the rough stuff," said Daniel.

Jem said casually, "How much d'yer want for it?"

Daniel didn't even know if he wanted to sell it, but upon consideration decided that money was more use than a ring and to sell it to Jem would be easier than explaining where it came from at the pawn shop.

"What d'yer reckon it's worth?" he asked, not wanting to commit himself.

"Well, it can't be a ruby, not if you found it in the rough stuff, more likely a garnet. I'll give yer ten bob for it."

It was a month's wages! Daniel was very tempted, but something made him hesitate, reluctant to part with a thing of beauty which he hadn't even had time to look at properly.

"What you want it for?" he asked to gain time while he considered Jem's offer. A sudden thought struck him. "Here, have you got a girlfriend? Is that why you're so mopey?"

If Jem had not been so brown, Daniel was sure he would have reddened. As it was he frowned crossly and said, "None of your business, young Daniel." And then more agreeably, but without conviction, added, "Thought I might give it to my Mum for her birthday."

"Come off it!" said Daniel disbelievingly. "She had her birthday last month and anyway, if she had any more rings, she wouldn't be able to draw a pint of ale."

It was true. Dora had always been vain about her small white hands and her rings served the double purpose of drawing attention to them and storing her savings where she could keep an eye on them.

Daniel looked at Jem through narrowed, speculative eyes. He had got a girlfriend, he decided, though he didn't want the word to get around . . . and he wanted the ring for her. He considered how this turn of events might be used to his own advantage. Jem was his friend, but first things came first, and as far as Daniel was concerned that meant getting himself on the *Windhawk*.

"You can have it for five bob," he said slowly and thoughtfully and then added in a rush, "if you get Punchy to take me on as cook and cabin boy."

Jem sighed and shook his head. "We've been through all that before, young Daniel," he said. "First off, you can't cook . . . "

"I help my Mum at home!"

"Helping your Mum is one thing: cooking good food for two hungry men on a coal stove in a heaving sea is quite different."

"But you could ask . . . "

"I have asked him, you know I have: he says you're too young and that's an end of it."

"You can have the ring for half a crown if you'll ask him again," Daniel lowered his terms, "and if he says yes, I'll . . . I'll give it to you for free! Oh please, Jem!"

Jem looked at him kindly and saw the desperation in his eyes. He said as gently as he could, "I'm sorry, Danny, but it's not on."

"Then you can't have the ring!"

Daniel's face set into mean cross lines and Jem, who could still remember the despair of being twelve — even while suffering the quite different despairs of being twenty — looked at him with sympathy and amusement.

Then he looked at the ring again. It was a simple thing, but the red stone flashed with the glint of a flame, like love and pain burning together. It said everything he felt towards Annie and he wanted it badly. Of course, it was only a garnet, no one would find a ruby in the rough stuff . . . but it glowed in his hand like a drop of his own heart's blood. He glanced sideways at Daniel, and saw the

23

stubborn set of his downturned mouth. Danny was his friend but first things came first, and as far as Jem was concerned that meant getting the ring for Annie. He resorted to low cunning.

"Look," he said, "I can't get you on the *Windhawk*, not until you're older and you've got a bit of experience, but I'll give you ten bob and I'll tell you someone who might take you on, someone who's desperate for a crew . . . his new mate joined the army last week."

"He'll only say I'm too young."

"Tell him you're fourteen and small for your age . . . "

"Who is it?"

"Oh no, that's part of the bargain, I don't say until you let me have the ring."

The hooter sounded from the brick field, calling the workers back to their job.

Daniel got to his feet but still hesitated.

"Will you ask him to take me on? I mean sort of recommend me?"

Jem looked wary. "No, I can't do that . . . I mean, it wouldn't help you . . . he doesn't get on too well with Punchy and me."

Daniel had a feeling that he was making a mistake: but ten bob was a month's wages and if there was any chance that this unknown Skipper would take him on . . .

Out of the corner of his eye he saw the unmistakable figure of Mr Jarvis in his old brown hat heading towards the piles of rough stuff. If he was late again, he might well be desperate for a job.

"All right," he said, "it's a deal."

Jem counted out ten shillings into his hand and pocketed the ring.

"Well," said Daniel, "who is it?"

Jem seemed to hesitate. Now that he had got his way, it suddenly felt like a mean trick to play on a friend.

"Who is it, Jem?"

Jem turned away, feeling embarrassed.

"It's . . . Batty Fred," he said. "Jimmy Purslove walked out on him after one trip: he said fighting in France would be easier."

"What? Batty Fred! You mean the *Blackbird*? 'Ere, that's not fair!" It was a cry of rage, and Jem suddenly found himself on the defensive.

"Now look, young Daniel," he said gruffly. "No one else is going to take you, you know that: you're too young and you've no experience. But Batty Fred might, because he can't get anyone else to sail with him," and as Daniel began to protest he went on, "You say you'd give anything to sail on the *Windhawk*, well maybe you're gonna have to serve your apprenticeship on the *Blackbird* whether you like it or not. Then when Punchy retires you'll have got a bit of experience and he might let me take you on."

But Daniel was too angry to admit the truth of what he said.

"Well, who wants to sail with *you*!" he shouted bitterly, and he stamped his way back to the rough-stuff pile, telling himself as he went that Jem had as good as stolen the ring from him, and he would never, ever, speak to him again.

Three

The Anchor and Hope was about half a mile beyond the brick field, along the lane that led past the rough-stuff piles down to the Old Ferry Hard. Its position at the end of a long spit of land with the brickworks on one side and the mud holes on the other gave it a mixed clientèle, which added considerably to the liveliness of its reputation. On the night after pay day when brickies from the Lower Field and the muddies from the Lower Saltings turned up in force, it was considered part of the general entertainment that, after downing astonishing quantities of Dora's good ale, the two rival factions should then hammer each other into an even more advanced state of insensibility before staggering home together the best of friends. From time to time things did get a little out of hand, then it was the task of the barge crews, with Punchy in the lead, to throw the offenders into the shallow waters of the tidal flats or, if it happened to be low tide, into the rich wet mud of the saltings. If Punchy was away on the *Windhawk*,

Dora was quite capable of leading the "chucking out" herself. With a rousing cry of, "Right, gentlemen! I've had enough!" she would wade determinedly into the ring leaders and after boxing their ears soundly would frog-march them to the door by the back of their collars. Since she was universally adored, and having one's ears boxed by Dora was the highlight of any man's evening, the happy offenders would bend obediently to have their collars firmly clasped, and more than one had been heard to call, "Thank you kindly, Mam," before hitting the mud face first.

In the long hot days of summer, the Anchor and Hope was much plagued by the flies from the rough stuff. Well gorged on the decaying refuse, they would arrive in swarms, each with an insatiable thirst, and proceed to behave in a manner quite as drunk and disorderly as that of the other regulars. For this reason it was customary for each man to sit with the palm of one hand covering his mug; this did not actually stop the marauders drowning themselves in the ale, but did reduce the number of the happy corpses. It was the proud boast of the pub's customers that when the flies settled on the window blind the sheer weight of their numbers pulled it down, and when you swatted them away the blind went up again.

Daniel, approaching down the dusty track after work that day, marvelled once again at the extraordinary shape of the building. The Anchor and Hope had been built out of old barge timbers and as a result was curved where any sane building would have been straight. This, and the fact that one end of it had settled rather deeper into the soft sand of the headland than the other, gave it a friendly, comfortable air, like an amiable drunk sleeping if off in the afternoon sunshine. Daniel had come in search of "Batty Fred", whose real name had once been Fred Batey but whose eccentricity had long since turned his name around and twisted it a little into its present universally recognized form. In his prime he had been perfectly normal, indeed he and Punchy Kitson had been the best of companions, both experienced barge Skippers, well matched and friendly rivals, until young Dora Midgeley had come into their lives. They, along with countless others, had both fallen hopelessly in love with her, and neither had ever recovered from the fall. Dora had been hard put to it to choose between them and being a kind-hearted girl, when she realized that Punchy was winning the battle for her affections, she had gone out of her way to be nice to Fred. She did this partly out of delicacy, to hide the growing strength of her feelings from the fortunate Punchy, and partly from a mistaken sense of pity, to conceal the awful truth from the unfortunate Fred. As a result, Fred Batey had been misled into believing that he was the favoured one and the sudden announcement of Dora and Punchy's engagement had thrown him into an abyss of despair from which he had never really emerged.

It was the central belief of his life that Punchy had stolen Dora from him, and with her (as if she were not loss enough) all hope of married joy, hearth and home, children upon his knee, and the ultimate blissful retirement to the good life of the Anchor and Hope. On the day when the engagement was announced, there had been a terrible fight between them. Punchy had won and Fred Batey had never spoken to him again. If he found it necessary to refer to him, Fred invariably called him

"Paunchy" Kitson, a libel which had become less libellous as the years went by. His hatred of the father was extended in due course to include the son, an antagonism which was only aggravated by the knowledge that Jem's skill as a sailorman grew as his own waned.

Towards Dora, Batty Fred remained as devoted as ever, insisting that the unspeakable Paunchy had led her astray. She, saddled with the knowledge that she had unwittingly brought him to this pitiful state, treated him with sympathy and forbearance, keeping his seat at one end of the bar, and agreeing with everything he said, and then making her way to the other end of the bar to be equally agreeable to Punchy and his friends. This remarkable charade had been going on for so long that the regular customers took it for granted. As for what the casual visitor made of it, well, what with the smell of the mud flats when the wind was in the east and the smell of the rough stuff when it was in the west and the flies which swarmed whichever way the wind blew, casual visitors at the Anchor and Hope were few, and those who did come, rarely stayed long enough to notice.

Daniel had spent half the afternoon seething with anger at the trick Jem had played on him. Everyone knew that Batty Fred couldn't keep a crew: his bad temper and his morose nature made him unbearable company in a two-man barge. Unlike most Skippers, who sailed under the flag of one of the big brick or cement companies, Batty Fred owned his own barge and was answerable to no one but himself. Having no wife or home or family to support he had put all his earnings into buying the *Blackbird*, but by the time she was paid for, his rudeness and independence had antagonized most of the company managers who might otherwise have employed him. As the years passed he made less and less money and the poor *Blackbird* grew steadily scruffier as he patched and mended her with makeshift repairs. Now she was reduced to the mud work, bringing in loads of the blue river mud which was added to the brick clay with a little chalk to give the bricks their distinctive colouring. To work with Batty Fred on the mud work was not Daniel's idea of life on a sailing barge, as Jem knew perfectly well.

But during the second half of the afternoon as his resentment faded, Daniel began to see the truth of what Jem had said. No one else would employ a boy of twelve or overlook the lie about his age. It was possible that even Batty Fred wouldn't want him. But if he did, if he could be persuaded . . . well, at least he would gain some experience, even if he was forced to get it the hard way.

He slipped in through the side door, taking a deep breath of mud-scented air into his lungs before plunging into the thick soupy fug which passed for air inside the Anchor and Hope. There was a theory that the smoking of coarse shag tobacco – which was stuffed into long clay pipes and smelt rather like old socks burning – helped to keep the flies at bay; but as far as Daniel could see they were as addicted to the pipe smoke as they were to the ale. They performed aerial acrobatics with a strident hum through the billowing clouds like tiny aeroplanes locked in combat, before finally plummeting with a screaming crescendo into the nearest unguarded ale mug.

The bar was packed, and Punchy was holding forth with a story of his racing days to a select crowd at the far end by the chimney corner.

"Well, I'm looking at them going down the river and

when we get to the end of that buoy, they're still goin' squared off; well, they ain't quite squared off, the wind was west-north-west, that's how the wind was." He paused for a mouthful of ale. "So I thought when they round the Spit they ain't gonna fetch the next buoy . . . foul tide, lee wind, y'see. My mate says to me, 'Where we goin' Punchy?' And I says, 'We're goin' through the Gat.' " There was a murmur of astonishment from his audience though they had heard the tale a hundred times. "So I 'as a look and the Black Grounds is still awash. So we're goin' across the Gat with a free sheet and when they go round the Spit, they've got to haul 'em up . . . they've got to haul 'em right up!" An appreciative burst of laughter followed this wily manoeuvre, for though the great barge races were only a memory the barge skippers still pitted their wits against each other all the time. Racing was a way of life, for the first man to complete a passage could unload and pick up a new freight before the last barge was moored up, and as they were paid by the freight, a fast Skipper was a wealthy one.

While Punchy warmed to his story, Daniel's roving eye spotted Jem's curly head bent over a side table beside the lank, dark hair of a man whose back was turned. He craned his neck sideways to see who it was, but when the man did turn his head it was the profile of a stranger.

"Well, we're goin' across free, a couple of points off the wind and then the fun starts: the *Coot* and the *Durham* don't fetch it!"

Daniel watched Jem and the dark-haired man resentfully and then as a gap opened in the throng he thought he caught sight of a gleam of red on the table between them. He saw the stranger raise his hand and in it the unmistakable white flash of a five pound note. Anger flooded him. Had Jem cheated him of his prize for a miserly ten shillings only to profit by his gullibility? He was only slightly mollified to see Jem shake his head stubbornly and thrust the ring back into his pocket.

"Well, they're about a quarter of a mile below, so they 'as to stand up on a starboard tack and while they're standing up. I nips through and away I goes . . . by the time they get round I'm two miles ahead of them!"

There was another burst of laughter, grunts of approval and banging of ale mugs on the table, which woke up the flies and sent the window blind rattling up.

It woke Daniel out of his trance and, remembering why he had come, he looked around for Batty Fred. It was not difficult to spot him in the black bowler hat, tarred against the weather, which had been the mark of the old barge captains before the turn of the century, and to which Batty Fred clung stubbornly to show his contempt for the Kitsons and their like, in their namby-pamby blue peaked caps. He was in his usual place at one end of the bar, chatting to Dora, who did her best to keep him occupied when Punchy was in full spate, lest one of his loud needling comments in the middle of the tale should provoke a punch-up before the customers had had time to drink their fill.

Daniel edged his way over, but Dora's eagle eye spotted him.

"What you doin' in here, young Daniel?" she asked sharply. "You're too young to be smoking and drinking. Go off home with you."

"I . . . I wanted a word with Mr Batty, I mean Mr Batey," said Daniel, getting off to a bad start in his confusion.

Dora softened. She could see that the end of Punchy's tale had been followed by a widespread emptying of mugs, and that her services would soon be in demand. She needed someone to distract Batty Fred.

"Well then, dear," she said sweetly, "you can just stay a moment and have a word with Fred while I'm busy; back in a moment."

And she sailed gracefully away down the length of the bar like a swan on the water, her white arms reaching out for the empty mugs as they came crowding up.

Batty Fred scowled at Daniel, convinced that he had somehow driven Dora away.

"What you want with me then?" he demanded, narrowing his eyes suspiciously.

Daniel took a deep breath to give himself courage and choked on the shag tobacco smoke. By the time he had finished a bad coughing fit he was red-eyed and hoarse of voice, but at least watching his discomforture had put Batty Fred into a slightly better mood.

"I heard you were needing a crew," croaked Daniel as soon as he could speak again.

A thin smile curved Batty Fred's mouth. "Why?" he said. "D'you know one?"

"It's me," said Daniel nervously and began to cough again.

Batty Fred's smile turned into a sneer of disbelief. "You?" he said. "You! Four-foot-nothing and a weak chest by the sound of it? Pull the other one, lad, it's got bells on!"

"I haven't got a weak chest," said Daniel indignantly, "it was just the smoke, or maybe I swallowed a fly, and I'm five-foot-two."

He wasn't, but it seemed unlikely that Batty Fred would have a tape measure on him.

" 'Ow old are yer?"

"Fourteen," lied Danny and as his conscience smote him he added, " . . . just."

Batty Fred sniffed scornfully. "I've seen a leg of mutton as was bigger," he said and turned away as if the conversation was closed.

But he did need a crew. It wasn't that he couldn't sail the *Blackbird* single-handed if need be, or at least with a little help from Joxer, his dog. Nowadays they only went back and forth around the headland from the brick field to the mud flats. But he hated cooking his own food at the end of the day and brewing his own tea, and he badly needed someone to take on the chore of scrubbing off the mud that clogged the deck and the shrouds after each loading.

The boy was still standing there, staring miserably at his feet.

"What you hanging around for, then?"

"I'm strong for my age," said Daniel hopefully.

"Can yer scrub decks?"

"Oh yes!" Daniel's face lit up. He had spent many a happy hour helping Jem with that chore.

"Can yer cook?"

"Er . . . yes." The voice was a little less certain.

"Make a mug of tea?"

"Course I can." He often did this at home when his mother was not too well.

"Humph!" There was another long silence.

"Make fast a mooring rope?"

"Yes!"

"Boom her out of a mud hole?"

"Yes!" said Daniel, who was not at all sure what this meant. It seemed to him from the string of questions that Batty Fred was weakening and he would have sworn recklessly to any skill if it would tip the balance in his favour.

"Humph!" Batty Fred seemed to lose interest.

Dora came bustling back and seemed surprised to see Daniel still there.

"Better go home now, luv!" she said crisply.

Daniel took his courage in both hands. "Mr Batey is giving me a job on the *Blackbird*," he told her eagerly, and seeing Batty Fred's scowl added nervously, ". . . I think."

Dora seemed surprised but generally approving. "Well, that's nice dear," she said. "He's a good lad by all accounts, Fred, even if he is only . . . "

"Fourteen!" said Daniel loudly.

Dora raised one high-arched eyebrow even higher and then winked at Danny, adding a new generation to the ranks of her devoted admirers.

". . . fourteen!" she concluded. "Still, he's a big lad for his age!"

It was patently untrue and Daniel knew she was teasing him, but he loved her for it. With Dora on his side, Batty Fred didn't stand a chance. Faced with her beaming smile of approval he capitulated.

"Orl right . . . 'arf a crown a week!" he growled crossly.

Daniel was overjoyed. It was as much as he got for picking rough stuff even though it was much less than a boy normally earned on the barges. But Dora came to his rescue. Before he could accept she said quickly, "All found, of course, Fred?"

Batty Fred, who had hoped to deduct Daniel's keep from the meagre sum, knew he was caught. He could never reveal to Dora the extent of his meanness.

"Yerse, all found," he agreed.

Daniel could hardly believe his good luck. "All found" meant that the whole half a crown could go home to his mother and Rosie. She might even be able to spare a few pence back for pocket money, a luxury he had never known in his twelve years so far.

"Shake on it then," said Dora firmly, making it impossible for Batty Fred to back out of his deal.

Daniel wiped his hand on his trousers and presented it to be shaken, though he need not have bothered since if anything Batty Fred's was the dirtier of the two.

"Right now. You go off home then, young Danny," said Dora, "and tell your Ma the good news."

"When do I start?" asked Daniel.

"Tomorrow morning, first light," said Batty Fred just to be awkward.

"Nonsense, Fred!" said Dora. "He'll have to tell old Mr Jarvis he's leaving. He'll start on Monday morning," she decided firmly, "if Mr Jarvis is willing," and with that she swanned away along the bar to deal with another empty pint.

Daniel and Batty Fred were left staring at each other. Dora seemed to have settled everything.

"Well, good night then," said Daniel politely. "I'll see you first thing on Monday morning."

But Batty Fred had the last word. He narrowed his eyes

to wicked little slits and with Dora safely out of earshot he hissed ominously, " 'arf a crown, all found, *less break-ages*."

Four

At an hour when all respectable folk were sound asleep in their beds, the *Windhawk* let go her mooring lines fore and aft and moved like a dark shadow away from the quay by the Lower Field and out into the smooth waters of the Medway. There was only a breath of wind but long years of experience told Punchy Kitson that it would strengthen into a good sailing breeze before the dawn. They had loaded a freight of Kent stock bricks for Chelsea, so he had timed their departure to catch the last of the ebb down the Medway. Then, out past Garrison point, they would heave-to off the Yantlet, if need be, to await the rising wind and flood tide which would speed them on their way up the Thames.

It was a moonlit night with passing cloud, and the *Windhawk* sang gently to herself as she moved down the black and silver river: her song made up of straining canvas, humming rigging and the sweet, joyful music of water rippling against her bows.

Jem and Punchy stood silently by the wheel, filled with the deep sense of satisfaction and excitement which never failed to move them when the quayside dwindled into the distance and another passage was under way.

"Young Daniel working overtime, is he?" said Punchy, his keen eyes catching a gleam of light against the dark, heaped mounds of the rough-stuff piles.

Jem followed the direction of his gesture and saw a second light beside the first. His eyes, younger and sharper, could just make out two figures outlined against the blackness of the pile, and his ears caught the faint crunching sound of the falling rough stuff in the damp emptiness of the night air. He narrowed his eyes and stared in silence for a while at the moving lights. If any suspicion crossed his mind as to who it might be and what they might be seeking in such an unpromising hunting ground, he kept his thoughts to himself.

"I doubt if it's young Daniel," he said. "I don't reckon his heart's in 'is work. On at me agin he was to get him a berth on the *Windhawk*."

Punchy laughed, but it was a sympathetic sound. "What you tell 'im?"

"Told 'im if he was dead set on joining the barges, he'd better ship with Batty Fred."

"You didn't, did you?" Punchy sounded quite shocked.

Jem grunted: he still felt guilty about it.

"Poor little perisher!" said Punchy. "Let's 'ope 'e's got more sense!" And he put the wheel over a fraction, tightening her up a little as they came round into Kethole Reach. They threaded their way between the looming shapes of the great battleships which lay at anchor there, and tacked into Salt Pan. As they passed the Blackstakes and came up towards Sheerness, they nearly ran down a small boat showing no light, which, though Punchy cursed its crew loudly and their fathers before them, gave no answer, but moved quietly on into the obscurity of the night. Punchy frowned. What with the lights on the rough-stuff piles where they should not have been, and boats without lights when they should have had them, he thought, it was probably best not to look too closely into the things that went on on the river during the hours of darkness.

By the time the first faint hint of light showed up the crowded horizon of the eastern sky, they were already through the Lower Hope, past Tilbury Docks and making the Long Reach up to Erith. Here they met with a stroke of luck. A tug coming up astern with a string of lighters in tow hooted a greeting, and Punchy recognized an old friend and colleague, "Tuggy" White. He waved back and shouted:

"Where yer bound for, Tuggy?"

"Brentford," came the reply across the water.

"Give us a tow to Chelsea?"

Tuggy grinned. "It'll cost yer half a crown."

"Have a heart," shouted Punchy, "I've got a wife and pub to support! Make it a florin."

"Done!" shouted Tuggy, "And a couple of pints next time I'm in the Anchor."

Once under tow, Jem and Punchy were able to lower the *Windhawk's* sails and spars as they went along to enable her to pass under the many Thames bridges between the Tower and Chelsea. And so it was that by the time the milkman was ladling the milk into the jug outside Number 17 Tadema Terrace, Chelsea, the *Windhawk* was alongside and mooring up at Chelsea Wharf.

Number 17 Tadema Terrace faced away from the Thames, turning its back fastidiously upon the noise and bustle of the river. It did its best to ignore the dubious smells that drifted up from the wharfside, where bricks were unloaded from the barges and the refuse from the smart Chelsea houses was dumped into the vacant holds.

From where Lily Tompkins stood, holding the jugs and flashing her brown eyes hopefully at the milkman's lad — who was too busy telling her about a German submarine which had been seen in the Thames only the night before to notice them — Tadema Terrace looked like any other quiet, respectable, tree-lined Chelsea street. It was, however, a source of constant embarrassment to Mrs Fanshaw, its mistress, that its rear windows presented an undesirable vista over the river and the railway siding.

It sometimes seemed to Beatrice Fanshaw that however hard she tried she only just managed to achieve social acceptability, and that it would take only a small set-back to bring her whole carefully constructed world tumbling down.

It had always irritated her that though her husband's name sounded superior enough, it was not spelt "Featherstonehaugh", for to possess a name like this, or "Cholmondeley" or "Mainwaring", which only the right people could even pronounce, had always seemed to her the acme of good breeding. It troubled her that though they lived in Chelsea, which was good, though not as good as Kensington, they did not live in the right part of Chelsea. It troubled her that though the front of her house was reasonably impressive, the back was not. And it troubled her that her two children, whom she had christened Charles and Elinor, and had endeavoured to bring up according to her own notions of perfect gentility, persisted in calling each other Charlie and Nora and seemed to have no interest in life beyond a fascination for the noisy, disreputable, passing scene of the London river.

Fortunately none of these failings troubled her children in the least, and while Lily was flirting with the milkman's boy and Jem was making fast the *Windhawk's* stern line, Charlie and Nora were leaning out of the nursery window at the back of Number 17 Tadema Terrace, waving ecstatically.

"I told you it was the *Windhawk*," crowed Charlie, leaning out as far as he could through the safety bars of the window. "You can't mistake her, even with her gear down; she's always the best."

"Can you see Jem?" Nora was breathless with excitement.

"Oh yes! Yes! There he is with the mooring rope. Oh quick! Quick! We must tell Annie."

At once they were down from the window sill and thundering down the stairs hollering, "Annie! Annie!" at the tops of their voices, so that poor Beatrice Fanshaw cringed at her dressing-table and wondered for the umpteenth time where she had gone wrong.

It didn't make things any better when her husband, Alfred, came stamping through from his dressing-room, where he had been making his usual mess of tying his tie, and said crossly:

"You'll have to do something about those two children, Beatrice!"

He had been saying this twice a week since Charlie was two and Nora was five, but had never once come up with any useful suggestions as to *what* she should do with them. If she pointed this out, he always said, "Well, you are their mother, you should know. You can't expect me to run your household for you, I've enough to do as it is running the Admiralty."

As he was in fact only a Second Assistant Under-Secretary or some such, and could hardly be said to "run the Admiralty", it was as well that he always beat a retreat into his dressing-room again before she could answer. Beatrice was much too well bred to shout after him, besides she was afraid that if she did, the servants would hear.

Charlie and Nora found Annie in the dining-room laying up the breakfast table. She had been engaged as a nursery maid when Nanny Parker, who had been with the Fanshaws for generations, became too old to cope with the children without supervision — though no one had the heart or the courage to tell her that she was too old. But as the Fanshaw finances did not really run to a nanny and a nursery maid, Annie also stood in for a number of other servants whom they could not afford. In fact it was her cheerful willingness to put on the housemaid's overall and make the beds, or dress herself up in lace cap and apron and play parlourmaid when her mistress's richer friends came to call, that made Beatrice overlook her undesirable connections. For although Annie was a sweet, natural and well-spoken girl, both her father and her grandfather had been sailing-barge Skippers. This might well have proved an insuperable obstacle in Mrs Fanshaw's eyes, but for the extenuating circumstance that they were both dead, as indeed was poor Annie's mother, leaving her an orphan alone in the world. She did have a legal guardian, her

Uncle Fred, and if the truth must be told, he was also a sailing-barge man. But by mutual agreement, Mrs Fanshaw and Annie never spoke about him.

Charlie managed to break the news first.

"Oh Annie, It's Jem. It's the *Windhawk*. They've just moored up to the quay."

"That's not fair, Charlie! I saw him first. I should have told her." Nora was most indignant.

"Well, I saw the *Windhawk* first, before you were even out of bed. I saw her as soon as she was past Battersea Bridge!"

"Oh, do hush!" said Annie anxiously. "Or I won't take you down there. Your mother would have a fit if she heard you. You know we are not supposed to have followers."

Nora got a fit of the giggles but did her best to giggle quietly.

"Oh Annie," she said in a delighted whisper, "how can you call Jem a 'follower'? It's such a silly name; he's just the most handsome man in all the world."

"Oh do hush, Miss Nora!" Annie who secretly thought just the same, was embarrassed by this open appraisal of Jem's good looks. She blushed as she thought of it and repeated, "Do hush your silliness or I'll take you round Brompton Cemetery for your morning walk."

"Oh, Annie, you wouldn't, you couldn't be so cruel!" Charlie clutched one hand to his heart and reeled as if struck by a mortal blow. "If you take me there, you'll have to leave me there. The disappointment would kill me!" And he dropped to the floor and lay motionless, his hands folded across his chest and an expression of angelic emptiness on his face.

Nora took some lilies out of the waxed-flower arrangement on the Chinese cabinet and tucked them between his hands.

Annie, laying the porridge spoons, came round the side of the table, saw him there and promptly got a fit of the giggles herself.

"Oh Master Charlie, you'll be the death of me!" she said.

"Promise to take us to the wharf then, or I'll lie here until mother comes in."

"Oh, all right, but do get up! I have to fetch the coffee up." And Annie hurried away down to the kitchen.

Charlie leapt up scattering lilies in all directions and with Nora in pursuit went thundering after her.

"Surely, Beatrice, it is not beyond your power to find a cook who can cook porridge without lumps in it," said Alfred Fanshaw a little later, crossly pushing the worst lumps to one side of his dish and abandoning them.

"She cooks a very good leg of mutton," said Beatrice defensively.

"That is no consolation at eight o'clock in the morning . . . and why has Annie taken to decorating the breakfast table with lilies?"

For some reason that he could not understand this remark threw Elinor and Charles into a fit of the snorts. He frowned at them forbiddingly.

Lily Tompkins came in with the bacon and eggs.

"Oh, Sir," she said, "what do you think? Those terrible Huns are lurking out there in the river in a submarino. The milkman says he spoke to a man who actually saw it. He was standing on Battersea Bridge last night, the man who saw it that is, not the milkman, and Cook says it's a disgrace and we shall all be murdered in our beds and what is the Admiralty doing about it?"

Alfred Fanshaw cast his eyes up to heaven in a gesture of long-suffering despair.

"It is not a 'submarino', it is a 'submarine', Lily," he said firmly, "and in any case it is not there, but if it were there, I can assure you that the Admiralty would have everything under control."

"Well, Cook's not so sure," said Lily ominously. "She says it's enough to give anyone an attack of the flutters and don't blame her if the porridge is lumpy!"

"It's all part of a fearsome Hunnish plot," said Charlie darkly. "They come up the Thames by night and put lumps in our porridge to give us all indigestion and break our resistance."

"Be quiet, Charles!" said Beatrice and Alfred in disapproving chorus.

Charlie shrugged and went back to bombing a large island of sugar with the convenient porridge lumps.

"The butcher's boy says there are spies everywhere," said Lily, "rowing up the river in boats without lights. I wouldn't be surprised if they come sneaking ashore just like Master Charlie says."

Charlie flashed her a smile of approval.

"Why is it," said Alfred Fanshaw scathingly, "that everyone in this house, not to mention the milkman and the butcher's boy, all think they know more about these things than I do? You all seem to forget that I work at the Admiralty."

But Lily remained unscathed.

"Cook says it stands to reason, the Admiralty would be the last to know, sitting around all day on their . . . that is to say, sitting behind their desks inside those offices.

Stands to reason, them as lives by the river would know whether they seen a submarino or not!"

"It was not a 'submarino', it was a 'submarine'!" said Alfred. "That is to say, it wasn't a submarine, but if it had been, it would have been . . ."

But Lily, taking advantage of his confusion, had swept out with the porridge dishes, thus ensuring, as always, that she had the last word.

Out of respect for old Nanny Parker's feelings, everyone at Number 17 Tadema Terrace always spoke as if it was she who took Charlie and Nora for their morning walk — as indeed she had taken them when they were babies and their father before them and his father before him. Nanny Parker even claimed to have pushed Great-Grandfather Fanshaw in his pram when she first joined the household as "a slip of a girl", and no one was in a position to argue with her, she being the sole survivor of those far-off halcyon days. Nor could the claim be contested by careful calculation of her age, since she had conveniently mislaid her birth certificate somewhere along the way.

All that the Fanshaws knew for certain was that she was somewhere between seventy and ninety and incapable of walking anywhere. Since she had pushed so many young Fanshaws in her time, it seemed only fair that Charlie and Nora should now push her in her antique bath chair, and so they did, though it must be admitted that they generally left it to Annie when they were going up hill. But they were only too willing to take over when there was a good down-hill slope, and they could play the exhilarating game of letting the bath chair run away by itself and pounding madly along in pursuit to catch it in the nick of time, just before Nanny Parker sped into the path of oncoming traffic or was catapulted over the embankment into the Thames. Since the old lady had not the slightest idea what went on behind her back, she endured these alarms and excursions with smiling equanimity.

Before they left the house, Mrs Fanshaw always instructed Nanny Parker to walk the children along the Chelsea Embankment or, if the weather were particularly fine, across the bridge to Battersea Park; and on their return she was always careful to question the old lady about the events of the outing. She did this to make quite sure that the children did not go anywhere near the wharf area, and she was always reassured by Nanny Parker's account of the trip.

What she did not know was that, once she had waved them out of sight and withdrawn into the house to rest from the pressures of the day, the bath-chair party would double back along Lots Road. Then they would settle Nanny Parker in a sheltered corner — where after a few mouthfuls of gin from the hip flask concealed under her tartan blanket, she would doze peacefully throughout the morning — and spend the rest of their outing in the company of the barge crews, all of whom had long been established as tried and trusted friends.

But it was the arrival of the *Windhawk* which gave their morning a particular golden glow. Charlie thought Punchy the best story-teller on the river, and would sit entranced by the hour listening to the exploits of his racing days, while Nora had been in love with Jem since she had first set eyes on him. Indeed, she had only brought herself to relinquish her claim on him in Annie's favour because the star-crossed tragedy of Jem Kitson and Annie Batey seemed to her like watching Romeo and Juliet played in earnest before her very eyes. For Annie had explained to her with many a tear brimming her wide blue eyes how, like the warring Montagues and Capulets, her uncle and sole guardian, Mr Fred Batey, had sworn such undying hostility towards Jem's father, Punchy, that even to ask his consent to their marriage was quite out of the question. The fact that the feud itself had arisen from yet another love tangle, between Punchy Kitson, Fred Batey and Jem's mother, Dora, left Nora almost speechless with envy. Not in her wildest dreams could she picture her own mother, Beatrice, as the object of such violent and enduring passion.

So, while the yellow Kent stocks were unloaded from the *Windhawk*'s hold, Charlie sat like a tableau of "The Boyhood of Raleigh" listening to Punchy's reminiscences, and Nora sat in a dream watching Jem and Annie play out their love story.

Not that they said much, or did much come to that. Nora would have enjoyed eavesdropping on long, impassioned speeches but neither of the lovers were given to making them.

Annie would say, "How's your Mum then?" and Jem after giving the question due thought would answer, "She's all right."

And then Annie would say, "How's my Uncle?" and Jem would sniff and say, "Bad as ever!" and they would sigh in unison.

Nora longed for passionate embraces, but again she was out of luck.

She could only watch with bated breath as their hands, carelessly resting on the forepeak hatch-cover where they sat side by side, crept imperceptibly closer.

But this morning was to mark a great landmark in the romance, the moment when Jem, still gazing absently out across the water as if hardly conscious of Annie's presence beside him, reached in his pocket and without a word laid on the brown hatch-top a gold ring with a red stone. Freed from the darkness of his pocket, it caught the afternoon sunlight and suddenly flashed fire.

If Nora had been Annie, she would have squealed with delight and seizing the ring tried its effect at once on the fourth finger of her left hand. But Annie made no move: she just went on sitting there, her head tilted slightly sideways so that she could see the ring out of the corner of her eye. And the fire that flashed from it seemed to light up her face with a slow, rosy blush. Jem's hand moved an inch or two pushing the ring a little closer to her so that she was forced to acknowledge it. The blush deepened.

"That for me, then?" she said with studied carelessness, just in case it might not be.

"I reckon so," said Jem, equally carelessly, adding after a moment's thought, "if you want it, that is."

The ring flashed and sparkled as if, like Nora, it was willing Annie to pick it up and try it on.

"That's a powerful fine ring," said Annie nervously. "Where d'you get that then?"

"That's for me to know and you to find out!" Jem used the traditional teasing answer to avoid telling her the unromantic truth that it had spent the last year or so lying among the decaying ruins of the rough-stuff pile.

There was another silence during which Annie's fingers stole out and touched the ring, turning it around and sending it into a frenzy of fire.

"Better put it on then," said Jem, "see if it fits."

Annie picked it up cautiously as if the red fire threatened to burn her fingers and, taking a deep breath to give her courage, began to slip it on to her right-hand ring finger.

"Wrong hand," said Jem succinctly.

"Left hand is for engagements," Annie's voice was so soft, it hardly reached Nora's straining ears.

"That's right."

"Oh, Jem!" said Annie, and with infinite caution she slipped the ring on to the fourth finger of her left hand, where it fitted perfectly.

("It was the most romantic scene I've ever watched," Nora told Charlie as they lay in their beds later that night. "Much more romantic than Romeo and Juliet!" But Charlie only buried his head in his pillow and said, "Sounds wet to me!")

When the time came to go home, they took their leave of Punchy and Jem, wheeled old Nanny Parker back up Lots Road, and chatted to her about the morning's events.

"Wasn't it lovely in the Park?" said Nora sweetly.

"Did we go to the Park?" the old lady frowned.

"Oh, Nanny Parker," said Charlie reproachfully, "you didn't drop off to sleep again did you?"

"Sleep! Of course not! I never sleep when I'm on duty. The Park was looking lovely!"

Charlie and Nora giggled cheerfully as they pushed her home, but they couldn't help noticing that Annie was much quieter than usual.

Five

Daniel left home in the early light of Monday morning
with his heart full of joy and his stomach churning
uneasily. After turning for the twentieth time to wave just
once more to the now tiny figure of Rosie, standing by the
house and clinging to the last sight of him, he turned the
corner away from the town and set out on the three-mile
walk to the quayside. He was glad to see that his mother
had kept her promise not to stand too long at the door, for
there was a fresh breeze and her cough was troublesome
again. He felt again a sense of guilt and unease at leaving
her.

Her first reaction to his exciting news had been one of
dismay. She had hoped to see him rise in the brickworks'
hierarchy to become a brick moulder like his father. She
even cherished a secret hope that, being a determined and
intelligent lad, he might move on to higher things. She
had great faith in her children and did not even consider
Mr Jarvis's shoes too big to fit her son in time.

Such ambitious thoughts would not have occurred to most of the brickworks' wives, but then Adela Swann was different. For a start she had not been bred in the brick fields like most of the others. She had been a Southend girl working in a smart milliner's shop when young Jack Swann, taking a day trip to the seaside on the *Medway Queen*, had encountered her on her Sunday off. It had been a love match and a happy marriage, but she had never really fitted in. The dampness and the cold wind on the saltings did not agree with her more delicate lungs and Jack had been forced to move her from the row of workers' cottages by the brick fields to the more sheltered streets of the small town a few miles inland. In so doing, he had separated Daniel and Rosie from the brickyard children who would otherwise have been their natural playmates and himself from the workmates who would have been his evening drinking companions. Not that Jack Swann had ever regretted the sacrifice. His parents had had their doubts, especially when Adela had given them grandchildren less solid and sturdy than they had hoped for; but Jack felt that what his son and daughter lacked in brawn they made up for in looks and intelligence. Old Mr and Mrs Swann had since died, and their son's family grew increasingly self-contained and separate from their neighbours, finding contentment enough in their own company until the misfortune of war had carried Jack away to France.

Breathing the wind from the sea into his own strong lungs, Daniel wondered if he had done right to leave his mother and Rosie. Would his father reproach him for it when he came home on leave? If Adela had pleaded with him to stay, he would probably have done so; but both she and Mr Jarvis, after pointing out to him the obvious advantages of a career in the brickyard, had seemed content to let him go. What Daniel could not know, of course, was that a secret conference between his mother and the brickyard manager had reached the conclusion that a few trips on the *Blackbird* with Batty Fred was just what Daniel needed to cure him for ever of his wild obsession with the barges.

"In a couple of weeks," Mr Jarvis had predicted confidently, "the lad will be back in my office wanting his job back. I shall give him a good lecture, Mrs Swann, and that will be the last you'll hear of this sailing lark. He'll settle down and follow in his father's footsteps, and you and I will look back on this day and laugh about it."

He had patted Adela's hand reassuringly and she, overwhelmed by his wisdom and forbearance, had felt almost presumptuous believing as she did that it was his shoes and not her husband's which her son was destined to fill.

But as home grew farther away and the quayside grew closer, Daniel consoled himself with the thought that he would never be far away on the mud work, and could keep an eye on his mother and Rosie on his day off. He rounded the last corner, and at once the sight of the *Blackbird* drove all other thoughts from his mind. She was not beautiful like the *Windhawk*, which had been built for barge racing in the old days, with fine lines and ample sails. The *Blackbird* was stumpy-rigged, without a top mast or the high topsail and flying jib that went with it. Her hull was smaller too, having been built originally to carry bricks up the Thames and through the canal locks as far as the Grand Junction. With her short black sail and her tubby black hull and her air of general neglect, she was known disrespectfully in the brickyard as the "Old Crow", but to Daniel's eyes she was the most welcome sight in the world. Indeed, if it had not been for the fact that Batty Fred went with her, he would have been content at that moment to ask for nothing more.

Daniel was not at all certain at what time he was expected to report for work, but fearing that if he misjudged the hour Batty Fred might take advantage of his absence to back out of the deal, he had risen before daylight for the long walk down to the quayside. But as he came close he saw that the *Blackbird* was deserted. He stepped cautiously on board and the slight sound of his footfall woke the ever-vigilant Joxer, who was up on deck in a moment, baring his teeth with a low, threatening growl. Daniel hastily stepped ashore again, deciding to wait at a safe distance. But the dog was not satisfied. He set up a ferocious barking intended to drive Daniel away, and grew increasingly hostile when he persisted in hanging around.

After a few minutes of this, while Daniel debated nervously whether to go or stay, there was a sudden angry cursing from below and the top half of Batty Fred emerged from the aft hatch. At five-thirty in the morning he was not a pretty sight, with red, bleary eyes, and a chin starting a rough growth of beard. He was wearing only the hard bowler hat, without which Daniel had never seen him, and a pair of frayed combinations of an indescribable colour somewhere between the yellow of aged wool and the grey of neglect. A general disregard for clean linen or personal hygiene was all part of Batty Fred's war against Punchy Kitson: it was his way of proving how low he had been brought by the loss of Dora and the discomfort it entailed had helped to keep the flames of resentment fanned within him over the long passage of years.

He glared balefully at Daniel.

"Get away from my ship, you little vandal!" he bellowed. "Before I set the dog on you."

"But Mr Batey, it's me, Daniel Swann."

"Never 'erd of yer," and the bowler hat sank again below the level of the hatch top.

"I'm your new crew, Mr Batey, don't you remember?"

The hat rose a foot or so until Batty Fred's mean red eyes were just visible above the hatch coaming.

"You're too small!" he said. "What would I be doing hiring a crew scarcely out of his nappies?"

"But you did hire me!" said Daniel desperately, and perceiving suddenly that the old man knew it quite well, and was only bent on tormenting him, he retaliated in the only way he knew.

"If you back out now, I shall go and tell Dora!" he threatened.

Batty Fred sniffed and seeing that he had exhausted the possibilities of teasing Daniel, he changed tack abruptly.

"Well, if I'm payin yer wages, why are you standin around idling?" he shouted. "Fill a bucket and give the deck a good scrub down, and get the mud off the standing rigging and be quick about it. You keep a good watch on 'im, Joxer," he added threateningly and went back to sleep for another hour.

Fortunately Daniel had not expected much kindness at Batty Fred's hands so the unenthusiastic welcome did not dampen his spirits. It was going to be a hot day and there was a faint haze over the flat waters of the Medway creeks.

The air smelt clean and salty and good enough to eat, and Daniel breathed in the familiar overtones of mud with a deep contentment. He filled and refilled the bucket, sluicing the grey-green water around and watching with satisfaction as his efforts dislodged the fine patina of old mud which seemed to cover the *Blackbird* from stem to stern. An hour later the sight of the clean wet wood beginning to dry off in the morning sunshine was balm to his soul. From where he stood he could see the rough-stuff pile, though the boys had not yet arrived, and the gentle movement of the barge timbers beneath his feet reminded him all the time that he had escaped from the daily grind of sifting and sorting, and that even if Batty Fred did his worst, from now on every day of his life would be a holiday.

Batty Fred did his worst.

By the time the *Blackbird* was ready to leave harbour, Daniel had scrubbed the deck, cleaned the standing rigging, washed up a week's pans and crockery, polished the iron stove and cleaned and trimmed the brass lamps. He was exhausted and hungry but refused to show it. He knew he could not stand the pace indefinitely, but he sensed, quite rightly, that Batty Fred was trying to get the better of him and a deep reluctance to be beaten gave him the energy to keep going.

At last Batty Fred relented and told him to brew up some tea. He produced some rather stale bread and cut off two hunks of it, dipping his own piece in the hot tea and eating it with loud sucking noises. Since Daniel had not inherited Adela's fastidious habits along with her other refinements, this did not worry him at all, in fact he tried it himself and found it improved the dry bread considerably.

By nine o'clock, the morning haze had cleared and a ripple on the water showed a little wind farther out in the creek. Batty Fred decided to tow the *Blackbird* out to it. Fastening a line to her bows he rowed ahead in the ship's dinghy, pulling the barge behind him at a snail's pace, while Daniel to his delight found himself entrusted with the wheel.

It was quite clear that the old man was not at all happy about this division of labour, but since even his strength was barely enough to move the *Blackbird*, and then only because she was a low-tonnage vessel and unladen, it was obvious to anyone that Daniel's small arms would be unequal to the task. The sight of his new crewman standing with beaming face at the wheel, while he strained his back in the dinghy, did nothing to improve the relationship between them.

Once out into the mouth of the creek, they picked up the breeze for the short passage and as, with the black sails hoisted and swelling with wind, they rounded the spit of land towards the Lower Saltings, Daniel felt that he had at last found his own particular heaven. He could see the Anchor and Hope in the distance dozing in the sunshine at the end of the headland, and he blessed Dora for taking a hand in his affairs. The richness of his satisfaction seemed to overflow on to all around him bringing Joxer, who had so far watched him with a mean suspicion, to settle comfortably by his feet. Even Batty Fred felt it and it made him uneasy. He had done his best to reduce Daniel to sulking and tears and the dratted child persisted in glowing with happiness as if he were on a day trip to the seaside. Fred decided gloomily that he was either very, very cunning . . . or he was barmy. Either way it made him an uncomfortable shipmate for one who had chosen misery and gloom as a way of life, and he would have to be got rid of as soon as possible.

They came round into the mud hole on the last of the flood and moored up to the marker buoy set by the muddies who dug the clay. There was no sign of them about, but a thin wisp of smoke rose from the iron chimney of the old stranded lighter they used as a refuge when the tide was in and the water over the mud holes made work impossible. Batty Fred's method of initiating Daniel into the special techniques of mooring, and preparing a barge for the mud work, seemed to consist of making it as hard as possible for the boy to find out what he was supposed to be doing, and then cussing at him for not doing it properly. The simple routines of putting a chain under the barge to break the suction if the weight of the clay should stick her in the mud; of putting out a kedge anchor on the deep-water side to edge her off the mud berth as the water rose; of stacking the hatch-covers and wrapping protective cloths around the mast case and the lower rigging: these were all accomplished with much muttering and shouting and cries of exasperation, when a few clear instructions about the purpose and nature of each operation would have made it possible for Daniel to be of some real assistance.

Daniel found himself wondering if Batty Fred was as stupid as he sometimes seemed or if he was just incurably mean and nasty. He began to see why the *Blackbird's* crews came and went with such unfailing regularity and in spite of the clear sunlit freshness of the morning, a faint cloud dimmed the brightness of his new life. To Batty Fred's deep satisfaction, a small anxious line appeared on

Daniel's forehead. But then Jake the Hermit arrived and everything changed.

Daniel saw him first emerging from the after hatch of the muddies' refuge: a broad stocky figure wearing a navy flannelette shirt, corduroy trousers held up by strong braces, high leather boots over-wrapped with protective padding, and a cloth cap. He surveyed the scene before him, scanning the sky for weather signs and sniffing the air knowledgeably like a good-humoured dog. Then, having tested the air and found it good, he took several deep breaths of it, raising his muscular arms and arching a back sorely tried by the constant bending of his craft. At full stretch he gave a loud triumphant cry of "Hah!" and picking up a pair of small wooden spades from the deck beside him, climbed purposefully down the ladder to the ground and came striding down the cinder path to the mud hole.

"A fine morning, *Blackbird*!"

The obvious good humour in his voice wiped the worried look from Daniel's face.

"Yes, isn't it," said Daniel, "It's my first day on the barges. I'm Daniel Swann."

"'Ello there! Fred got a new crew 'as 'e? What happened to Jimmy Purslove?"

"Gone for a soldier," Daniel explained.

"And glad of it, I shouldn't wonder." As he talked he was using one of the odd little wooden spades to clear the wet surface mud from the clay. The mud hole was dug out in a series of ledges so that digging could begin as soon as the tide dropped a few feet and the highest was uncovered. When the clay beneath his feet was clear enough to give a firm foot-hold he picked up the second spade, which was flatter than the first, and grinned up at Daniel, who was standing on the foredeck well clear of the main hold.

"If you stand there lad," he said, "you're like to get a good spadeful of mud in your ear."

Startled, Daniel glanced about him.

"I thought there would be a whole gang of you," he said, "shovelling it into the hold."

"Ah well, you see, I'm the 'Ermit." Jake gave him a knowing wink. "It's my job to fill the forehold first to get her bow well down."

Daniel thought fast as he moved out of the way, embarrassed at having been caught out.

"Oh, of course," he said as he suddenly saw the sense of it, "to keep the weight off the rudder."

"Ha! Well done, lad! You've got a sharp one there, Fred."

But Batty Fred only scowled.

"Wants to watch out 'e don't cut 'imself then!" he sniffed and as he stumped off down below he added, "and he talks too much."

Jake winked at Daniel in a friendly, conspiratorial way, making it clear that the old man's ill-humour was a joke between them, and then with apparently effortless ease he began to dig the clay. With astonishing speed he sliced into each heavy spit and tossed it in one continuous movement in a graceful arching curve straight into the forehold. Daniel watched fascinated, but not for long. Batty Fred's mean little eyes emerged again above the rim of the after hatch and glared at him.

"You think I pay you to watch other people work?" he demanded.

Daniel jumped.

"Sorry," he said. "Was there something to do?"

"Was there something to do?" Batty Fred did a high-pitched imitation of the innocent question. "Of course there's something to do, there's always work to be done on a barge and I'm paying you to do it. So you can get a bucket of water and start cleaning out down below."

For the next couple of hours Daniel scrubbed away at a floor which had obviously not seen a scrubbing brush in a very long time. It confirmed his suspicions that the endless hard work was not the result of Batty Fred's high standards, but was simply his device for making his new crewman as miserable as possible. But he had bargained without Daniel's pleasure in rescuing the *Blackbird* from the dirt and neglect into which her Skipper's apathy had sunk her. He felt for her in her sorry state as if she were a living creature, and he scrubbed the accumulated dirt of ages from her floors and cabin walls rather as he would have brushed and groomed a neglected dog. When the job was done, he felt tired and aching and a little light-headed with hunger, but he knew the job was well done, and he patted the *Blackbird's* clean damp woodwork affectionately, before rising to his feet and climbing up on deck to empty the bucket.

By now the mud hole was a hive of activity. There were eight muddies all dressed like Hermit Jake and all working together to load the main hold. They moved in unison like an efficient machine and the air was full of flying mud. So fast and smoothly did each man work that, before one spit of clay had hit the hold, the next one had already left the same spade.

The ganger in charge looked up as Daniel appeared.

"Ah lad!" he called, without ceasing in the rhythm of his work. "We thought you'd never show up. It's high time you brewed us all a mug of tea."

"Oh, I'm sorry!" said Daniel, feeling guilty that his enthusiasm for the *Blackbird*'s spring-clean had made him overlook the workmen's thirst. "Batty Fred . . . I mean, Mr Batey didn't tell me . . . " He glanced around wondering why the Skipper had overlooked an obvious opportunity to nag at him, and realized that the old man was nowhere to be seen.

The ganger saw his searching eyes and laughed.

"No use looking for old Fred," he said. "He's in our carsey."

He jerked his head in the direction of a small building which stood all alone a short way from the muddies' boat, and looking at it more closely, Daniel saw it was made from half a boat up-ended, with wooden doors on what looked like leather hinges.

"Should I wait until he comes?" asked Daniel dubiously, reluctant to brew the tea without Fred's instructions.

"No, no, lad! You get on with it. He'll just have forgotten to tell you; took short I shouldn't wonder."

"Well . . . " Daniel thought it must be all right if the ganger said so. One of the other muddies joined in.

"He'll be there for the next hour at least, reading his way through the newspaper squares hanging behind the door. He's too mean to buy his own paper, you see!"

"He sometimes spends the whole morning in there," added another.

"Oh, all right then," said Daniel and went below to brew up.

He could quite see the attraction of the muddies'

"carsey", primitive though it was, since none of the barges, even well-found ships like the *Windhawk*, had any kind of lavatory on board. When nature called, the crews were forced to lower a bucket into the sea, half-fill it with water and use it down in the fo'c'sle before emptying it down wind over the side. It was no fun balancing on a bucket with a cold wet rim on one side and a handle and a wet rope attached to the other. Daniel made a mental note to pay a visit to the upturned boat himself before they left the saltings.

Soon the old kettle began to sing on the iron stove, and he hunted around for cups and mugs. He remembered seeing four or five, mostly with chips and cracks, when he had washed up early that morning (it seemed like half a lifetime ago). To these he added a jug, a bent pewter mug, and something which could have been a small vase or a large beaker. He brewed the tea hot and strong with plenty of sugar and then made his way carefully up on to the deck, carrying the motley collection of containers on an old tin tray.

The muddies came swarming up to the boat, big and sweaty and cheerful.

"I don't know what Mr Batey usually gives you your tea in," said Daniel apologetically, "but I could only find five proper mugs."

This remark seemed to generate a great deal of good humour among the muddies, who laughed and slapped each other on the back and after tasting the hot sweet draught said they had never enjoyed a cup of tea so much in their lives. They said it with such sincerity and repeated it so often as they climbed back down into the mud hole, that Daniel began to feel distinctly pleased with himself as he piled the crockery back on to the tray and prepared to go below and wash up.

And then, just as the line of muddies bent their backs again for the first spadeful of mud and Daniel stood poised at the top of the companionway, there came a sudden bellow of rage from the direction of the little hut: Batty Fred, emerging at last into the sunlight, had just caught sight of Daniel and the loaded tray. Unfortunately, the interruption brought all the muddies' heads round in the direction of the sound and the sudden movement spoilt their aim. Eight spits of mud went soaring through the air, each one a little too far to the right, and the end one caught Daniel in the small of the back. He pitched forward, throwing out one hand to save his balance: the cups, mugs, jug and vase slid sideways with a rush and vanished down the hatchway with a shattering crash.

Six

Daniel was in a state of deepest gloom. Batty Fred's rage at finding all his dilapidated crockery in pieces had been terrible to behold and the full significance of those ominous words "less breakages" became terribly clear. Not only was the cost of replacing all the damaged items to be deducted from Daniel's meagre wages, but also the cost of the tea and the milk and the sugar consumed by the muddies. For now, all too late, he discovered that Batty Fred never gave them so much as a drink of water; that he even resented any time which they took off to brew their own. Now Daniel understood the reason for the muddies' great good humour as they consumed his offerings: it was the knowledge that they were putting one over on old Batty Fred that had made the tea taste so very good. He couldn't even find it in his heart to resent the trick they had played on him, for it had only been part of a well-deserved retaliation against Batty Fred's meanness, and they were not to know that the full force of his revenge would fall on

Daniel's head. Indeed the old man had been careful to vent his anger in the privacy of the cabin, perhaps fearing that if he did so in front of the muddies, they would intervene on the boy's behalf.

The only consolation to be found in the whole wretched incident was that Daniel had not actually been sacked. But Batty Fred made it quite clear that he would keep him on only so that there would be some wages from which the breakage money could be deducted.

The barge was fully loaded and the rising tide lifted her clear of the clinging mud, but there was no sign of wind in the mud hole. Batty Fred decided to boom her out.

Daniel had seen the manoeuvre carried out on more than one occasion by Jem and Punchy, and it had always looked quite simple. It involved the use of a long pole called a setting-boom, with which the barge was propelled along rather like the punts on the upper reaches of the river. But appearances were deceptive, and Daniel had considerably underestimated both the weight of the barge and the depth and clinging stickiness of the river mud. He did not like to ask for instructions, having rashly laid claim to experience at this particular skill when applying for his job, and Batty Fred's only advice was, "Put your weight into it, lad, and whatever you do, *don't let go of the boom!*"

Daniel carried the long pole to the front of the *Blackbird* and thrust it deep into the yielding mud until it held firm. Then he began to walk towards the back of the barge, pushing with all his strength against the setting-boom, so that the barge moved forward as he progressed from stem to stern. Once the barge had gained momentum, it was easier than he had expected and he began to feel quite pleased with himself . . . until he reached the point when the boom was to be plucked from the muddy depths and carried for'ard to repeat the whole manoeuvre. Daniel clutched at the boom, only to find to his dismay that it refused to come out. It did not even begin to move against the powerful suction of the mud and he knew at once, with awful certainty, that his slight strength would not be enough to free it. He was already at the stern of the barge, which was moving smoothly forward at a fair pace. There was no time to decide on the best course of action. The moment of decision came and with Batty Fred's cry of "*Don't let go of the boom*" still ringing in his ears, Daniel hung on to the pole with all his strength, thinking to bring the barge to a halt. But his strength was as nothing compared to the powerful weight of the moving barge, and the *Blackbird* slipped, silent and dream-like, out from beneath his feet, leaving him high in mid-air, still clinging to the pole above the wide expanse of mud and water.

For what seemed like an eternity, Daniel clung to the top of the boom like a monkey on a stick and stared disbelievingly at the picture of Batty Fred, incoherent with rage, leaping about on the stern of the *Blackbird* as the rising puff of wind caught her sail and moved her smoothly away down the creek. As if in some awful nightmare in which he was powerless to move and heard sounds only indistinctly, he listened to the old man's angry tirade, the gist of which was that Daniel was the most useless, incompetent and witless boy it had ever been his misfortune to encounter; that he was sacked as from that instant, breakages or no breakages; and that if Batty Fred never set eyes on him again, it would be too soon.

Daniel heard it all in a bemused silence, clinging to the

top of his pole, and then, still without a sound, he began to fall sideways, slowly at first and then with gathering momentum, as the rich, dark-grey mud of the saltings came up to meet him.

He was rescued by the muddies. When they had finally finished laughing and were able to stand again without supporting each other, they came wading out through the thick ooze, lifted Daniel's unrecognizable grey shape from its watery bed, pulled the precious boom from the grip of the deep clay, and with joyful tears of mirth still running down their happy red faces, carried them both back to the shelter and safety of their stranded lighter.

The thick, caked mud on his face made it impossible for Daniel either to laugh or cry, which was just as well for he would have been at a loss to know which to do. Even through the awfulness of his situation he could see that to an onlooker the whole thing must have been very funny; certainly, like the incident of the tea, it had given the good-natured muddies a great deal of pleasure. But quite apart from the sheer discomfort of his predicament, it seemed to be the end of all his hopes of a sailing life, which made him feel that from his own point of view tears would be more appropriate.

But they gave him no time to shed them. They stood him on deck and sluiced off the worst of the mud with buckets of salt water. Then they stripped off his clothes to be washed out, wrapped him in an old blanket and bundled him below. It wasn't a chilly day, far from it, but shock and the splash of cold water had given Daniel the shivers and he huddled gratefully beside the squat, fat-bellied iron stove which they used for cooking.

"Now lad," said Jake the Hermit, picking up a heavy

iron frying pan, "what you'll be needing is a good hot meal. I'll bet that mean old skinflint Batty Fred don't overfeed you."

Daniel realized that he was indeed very hungry. He nodded his head and tried to say, "Thank you," but the warmth and kindness seemed suddenly to release the tears which through the shock and the discomfort he had managed to keep in check. He tried to sniff them back but they continued to roll silently down his cheek.

" 'Ere, what's the trouble then, lad?"

Daniel shook his head silently, unwilling to explain, knowing that if he did, he would be making them share the blame for his misfortunes. But it was no use. They came crowding round in an anxious, friendly circle and made him tell the whole story bit by bit. Then they sat silently, deep in thought while the pan spat and sizzled on the stove.

At last the ganger said rather gruffly:

"Well, it would seem we've had a good laugh, lads, and now we shall have to put things to rights. You shall sleep here tonight, and we'll be off down to the Anchor to see Dora and find out what's best to do. And as for the breakages," he took off his greasy cap and poking deep into the pocket of his corduroys pulled out a couple of coins which he dropped into it. Then he passed the cap on to the nearest man and said, "I reckon a cup of Batty Fred's tea was worth paying for and if each man puts in the price of a good laugh, we'll soon settle our account."

There was a general murmur of agreement and the coins came rattling in. One of the muddies threw in an extra one saying:

"That's for the monkey up the pole. I've wanted to see

that happen for years, every time I've watched a barge boomed out of the mud hole, and I reckon it was worth as much as Batty Fred's tea . . . no offence meant, youngster!"

"None taken, I'm sure," said Daniel politely, as the memory of his exploit with the setting-boom brought a new shower of small change.

When the bulging cap was finally emptied into the folds of the blanket on Daniel's lap, it was clear that there was more than enough to satisfy Batty Fred's account.

"It's too much," said Daniel, staring down incredulously at the heap of pennies and sixpences in his lap. "I can't take all that."

"Buy a present for your Mum and your little sister then," said the ganger. "Sailors always bring back presents when they've been to sea." And before Daniel could argue he banged the pan on the stove and announced, "Grub up!"

Two hours later Daniel was all alone in the muddies' barge. Warm, full up and sleepy, he was dozily reviewing his many changes of fortune during the day and wondering if life on the barges was always so exhaustingly eventful. It was evening and the muddies had departed to the Anchor before going on to their homes in the row of cottages beyond the saltings. Only Hermit Jake would be returning for the night. He, true to his name, lived aboard the old lighter and kept the stove going. For the muddies' working hours were governed not by the clock but by the tide, and when low tide came early in the morning, they would be digging as soon as the light broke.

Daniel looked around the old refuge. The light of the stove and the few beams of late sunlight through the tiny port-hole windows showed a smoke-blackened ceiling hung with strings of dried mushrooms, a clothes line where his own clothes had almost finished steaming, and other odds and ends collected from the tideline along the foreshore. Stacks of driftwood dried by the stove, in which it burned with a blue salty flame. A basket held wild-duck eggs, which with bread, cheese and the mushrooms had formed the bulk of their hearty meal. But even as he surveyed the delights of this newly found paradise, tiredness overcame him. One moment he was watching the firelight on a string of green glass net floats and the next his eyes were closed. Two minutes later, he was fast asleep.

He was woken by a thin beam of morning sunlight and a strong smell of frying bacon. It took him a moment or two to remember where he was; then, as the memory of the previous day's events came flooding back, he was suddenly wide awake and sitting up and the sound of his movements brought a cheerful, "Morning, lad," from the big figure of Hermit Jake busy at the stove.

He paused in his cooking to pull down Daniel's clothes from the line and throw them across to him: they were warm and dry and smelt deliciously of mushrooms and bacon.

Over breakfast Hermit Jake told Daniel what had passed at the Anchor and Hope the night before.

"No problem, lad!" he said cheerfully, his mouth full of bread and bacon. "First, we bought him a few drinks — never say no to a drink won't old Fred, don't care who's buying it. Besides, I reckon he thought he was getting his own back for the tea. Then, when he wasn't thinking too clearly, we told Dora how well he was looking after you. Said he was like a father to you. Well, Dora was so pleased she came over all sentimental and told him he should have had a family of his own. And then, of course, he was well away: he ran through the whole maudlin story of how Punchy Kitson had ruined his life and done him out of his kith and kin, and what with Dora sympathizing and saying as how you must be like the son he never had, well, we carried him back to the *Blackbird* singing mournful songs all the way. With any luck, lad, he'll be round here on the first tide, trying to get you back, before Dora rumbles him for the mean-hearted, two-faced, old phoney that he really is."

And so it turned out. As *Blackbird* came up the creek and tied up to the mud hole, Daniel was waiting on the shore with the setting-boom in his hand. According to his instructions, he smiled innocently and called, "I didn't let go of the boom, Mr Batey, I kept it safe, just like you told me to."

Batty Fred smiled back, at least he tried to, but it didn't come easily. His face contorted into something between the grin of a toothy skull and the lip-curling snarl of a nervous dog.

"Well done, lad," he said, with a syrupy attempt at good humour which was rather less pleasant than his usual bad temper. "You'll soon get the knack of it." And to relieve his feelings he took a sharp kick at Joxer, who had completely gone over to the enemy camp and was greeting Daniel with an enthusiastic tail and sharp barks of joy.

Nothing more was said. Daniel climbed back on board, stowed the setting-boom and took up his duties where he had left them off, preparing the *Blackbird* for the arrival of his new-found friends, the muddies.

Seven

Daniel made his way along the road to the town in high good humour. A warm but blustery wind had sprung up, tossing the crows about the sky like old rags and driving a fine summer rain against his face, but nothing could dampen his spirits. It was Sunday lunchtime and he was on his way home.

He had hoped to spend the whole day with his mother and Rosie, but Batty Fred had come rolling home from the Anchor late on Saturday night and had snored noisily through most of Sunday morning, so that Daniel had been afraid to wake him to ask permission to go ashore. He had managed to get through the rest of the week without further disasters and although Fred had kept all his first week's pay to cover the breakages, Daniel had enough money from the muddies' collection to give his mother a week's money and something over to buy presents with. He would have liked to return laden with gifts, but there were no shops between the brickyard and the mud hole.

Still, he carried a rush basket of wild duck eggs as a present from the muddies and he was hoping to find the little corner shop still open — it opened for papers on Sunday morning — so that he could buy some sweets for Rosie.

As he tramped along in the steadily falling haze of rain, he could not but think that his first week had gone rather well. Whether from some change of heart or for devious reasons of his own, or even in an attempt to live up to Dora's picture of him as a second father to Daniel, there was no doubt that Batty Fred had been nicer to him after the incident with the setting-boom. Which was not to say that the old man had smiled or spoken to him kindly: not at all, he had remained as rude and surly as ever, but he had eased up a little on the endless succession of chores, and instead of criticizing the results of Daniel's best efforts, he just frowned at them and said, "Humph!" in a non-committal sort of way.

In Daniel's eyes this was a distinct improvement and there were even wild moments when he imagined that Batty Fred was on the point of saying, "Well done, lad," though it had never happened yet. But he felt that he could honestly report to his mother that he was making a success of his new life, and he cherished the observation passed by Mr Jarvis in his hearing that, "The old *Blackbird* is looking a sight cleaner these days, Mr Batey!" Unfortunately he had spoiled it by adding, "And not before time", which had not improved the temper of the *Blackbird*'s Skipper.

He reached the corner shop just in time to see old Mr Cooper pulling down the blinds. He rapped hastily on the glass of the door but a firm voice from the other side said,

"It's too late, lad, my dinner is on the table."

"Oh, please, Mr Cooper, it's me, Daniel Swann, I just want a few sweets for Rosie."

The blind shot up a few inches while Mr Cooper checked to see if this was true. Finding it was, he opened the door and said, "Quickly then, lad, or my missus will have my guts for garters!"

Daniel chose some mint humbugs in a fancy tin designed for an after-life as a tea caddy, thus providing him with two presents in one.

"They sent for you because of your Ma then, did they?" said Mr Cooper solicitously, as he rang up the money in the big brass till.

"Sent for me . . . " said Daniel uneasily, "why should they send for me?"

Mr Cooper looked at him oddly. "Well, she's sick, ain't she? . . . taking her away to the hospital, I heard . . . "

Daniel felt suddenly cold. With a hurried word of thanks he had grabbed the tin and his change and was running down the street towards home. As he went he said over and over to himself, "I shouldn't have left them, it's all my fault. I should never have left them . . . "

He reached the corner just in time to see the ambulance leaving the door. He shouted, but just as he did so the driver whipped up the horses and the sound of his cries was drowned by the clattering of hooves and the rumbling of wheels over the cobbles. Seeing that it was hopeless to try to overtake it, he lent against the wall, fighting to get his breath back and to keep the tears at bay. Then he remembered Rosie and began to run again, dreading to find that she had also gone.

Rosie was sitting in the front hall. She had a small

76

basket of clothes beside her with an old rag doll on top. Her face was white and staring and her eyes blank with fear and loss. She made no movement as Daniel's shape blocked the light of the doorway, only stared in front of her while one small thumb twisted the hem of her pinafore.

"Rosie?" In a moment Daniel was on his knees beside her. "Rosie! It's me, Daniel!"

Slowly she lifted her round, dark, empty eyes and seemed to look right through him.

"Rosie!" It was a cry of despair. He put his arms around her, hugging her tightly and suddenly she seemed to see him for the first time. Her white face crumpled up and she burst into a torrent of tears and clung to him desperately.

"They've taken Ma away, Danny . . . she wouldn't talk to me; she didn't look a bit like Ma . . . they're coming to take me away to the orphanage . . . does that mean Ma is going to die, Danny? Oh Danny, please don't let them take me away!"

"Hush," said Daniel, "hush, Rosie. Everything's gonna be all right. I'll look after you now, Rosie. I won't let anyone take you to the orphanage . . . "

"Promise, Danny, promise you won't let them take me!"

"I promise . . . now do stop crying. Look what I brought for you." He loosened her clinging hands and put the humbug tin into them, noticing as he did so that it celebrated the Coronation several years before. King George and Queen Alexandra stared out impassively at the scene of fear and anguish taking place around them. Daniel wondered if humbugs improved with time like wine and Christmas puddings.

But there was no time to find out. If "they" were coming to take Rosie to the orphanage, it was important that the two of them should be gone before "they" arrived. It did not occur to Daniel that his sister's stay at the orphanage might be a temporary measure until his mother should recover and return from hospital. Nor, indeed, did he feel at all certain that his mother would ever return. His world was a small one, bounded by the orchards to the south of his home town and the salt flats and the river to the north. He had no idea where "the hospital" or "the orphanage" might be, but they were certainly somewhere beyond the limits of the known world. Perhaps if he prayed hard enough his mother might one day return in the same mysterious way that she had been spirited away, just as his father had gone long before to the war, with no certainty of returning. Now there was only Rosie left and no one was going to take her away, white-faced and tearful and even more bewildered than he was himself, to some far-away orphanage where he might never find her again.

It was no use staying at the house. When "they" came, "they" would say a twelve-year-old was too young to look after his sister: "they" might even try to send him to the orphanage too! The very idea was enough to speed him on his way. He made a quick trip to the larder, but as his mother had been seriously ill for several days he found only some dry bread and a hunk of cheese. He stuffed these into his pockets, locked the doors so that all would be safe until someone returned, picked up Rosie's basket and taking her hand said, with a confidence he was far from feeling, "Now, you come with me, young Rosie, and everything will be just fine."

"Where are we going?" asked Rosie, brightening a little

at the prospect of this new adventure.

Daniel was not at all sure.

"Have a humbug," he said, knowing that this would make conversation difficult, and for a while they plodded on through the rain with only the sound of their wet shoes in the soft mud of the lane and the occasional loud sucking noises. Daniel searched his head for an answer to Rosie's question. They were going in the direction of the *Blackbird*, but was he really planning to take Rosie back on board with him? Did he imagine for one moment that Batty Fred would suddenly be filled with the milk of human kindness, when he learned of Rosie's plight, and would welcome her on board? He knew very well that it was nonsense. Batty Fred would throw them both out without a second thought, and then where would they go?

He finished his humbug slightly ahead of Rosie and, as she opened her mouth to repeat her question, he said carefully, "You are going to have to be very clever, Rosie, in fact I don't know any other little girl of seven who would be clever enough to do what you've got to do."

Rosie looked very important and said, "Can I have another humbug?"

And as they went on down the road, Daniel explained to her that he was taking her to live with him on board the *Blackbird*, but that Batty Fred must not find out, and that she would have to stay as quiet as a mouse and play a sort of game of hide and seek if ever Batty Fred came anywhere near the fo'c'sle.

Fortunately Rosie was a great hide-and-seek enthusiast, and the idea of playing the game for real rather appealed to her. Still she understood that the penalty for being caught would also be real and with uneasy visions of being

keel-hauled or made to walk the plank — standard penal-
ties in the pirate stories she begged from Daniel — she
asked rather anxiously, "What will happen if I get
caught?"

Daniel thought Batty Fred would probably have a fit
but he said casually, "Oh, he'll just put us ashore and we
shall have to find somewhere else."

Rosie looked disappointed. "Shan't we have to walk the
plank?"

"I might have to," Daniel compromised. "Girls don't
have to walk the plank."

"That's not fair," Rosie was most put out at this
discrimination. "I want to walk the plank, too."

"But you can't swim," said Daniel reasonably.

"You could rescue me!"

"Well anyway, we're neither of us going to have to walk
the plank, because you're not going to get caught, because
you're too clever!"

"That's true," said Rosie philosophically, "still, it
would have been fun!"

Daniel settled Rosie in a sheltered corner of the
brickyard with a great cowl of warm bricks to keep off the
wind and fine rain, and went cautiously down to see if
Batty Fred was still on board. He did not want to arouse
the old man's suspicions by his untimely return, so he
hung around at a distance watching for signs of life. Joxer
was lying unseen by the windlass, but, catching some
slight sound, jumped up and began to bark a welcome.
Hastily Daniel stepped back out of sight, but the sound
brought an ill-tempered shout from below deck which told
him all that he needed to know.

He returned to Rosie and they ate their way through the

bread and cheese and half the humbugs — which did seem to have matured with the passing years — while they watched the lane past the rough stuff for the sight of Batty Fred setting out for the Anchor and Hope.

Though the sky was dark with low racing clouds and the light rain fell steadily, the corner where they sat was warm and dry. Behind them the great cowl of newly fired bricks was slowly cooling: it had taken several weeks to burn right through, and would be another week before the bricks were cool enough to handle so that the cowl could be dismantled and the brick sorting could begin. In the meantime the heat that rose from it dried the air and carried the wind up and over the lee-side where Daniel and Rosie sat, as snug as they might have done by their own fireside.

Daniel was suddenly aware of a figure moving past the rough stuff and glanced up to see if it was Batty Fred. But it wasn't: it was a younger man in a dark-blue jacket, and as Daniel watched he moved off the path and into the space between the piles. There was something familiar about him though Daniel could not place the face in his memory. His movements were oddly furtive, which set Daniel wondering just what he was up to, for none of the brickyard employees would be around the rough stuff heaps on a wet Sunday evening.

"Stay here. I'll be back in a moment," he said to Rosie, and went round the side of the brick cowl to approach the rough stuff from the far side unseen. As he made his way cautiously along behind the piles Rosie's voice, close behind him, said suddenly, "Where are we going?"

He spun round. "I thought I told you to stay by the cowl," he hissed.

"I didn't want to," she hissed back. "I wanted to see what you were going to do."

"Well, I wanted to see what that fellow was up to, sneaking around the rough stuff. He looked as if he was up to no . . . "

But at that moment he was stopped in mid-sentence by a large dirty hand which came from behind and covered his mouth and another matching hand dealt with Rosie in the same way. They felt themselves clasped by strong unfriendly arms and as they struggled against the unseen assailant, a voice close by their ears said softly, "Keep still and keep quiet or I'll bang your heads together."

A long pause followed in which the only sound was the tread of feet along the path, and through a narrow gap between the heaps, Daniel saw Batty Fred shuffling his way towards the Anchor and Hope for another night's drinking.

When the footsteps had died in the distance, the pressure of the evil-smelling hand was eased a little and a threatening voice said, "What you doin' spying on me then, you perishing little brats?" The hard face under the lank dark hair peered closer at Daniel. " 'Ere aren't you the lad that found the . . . " But the question ended in a cry of pain as Rosie, taking advantage of the loosened grasp sank her small sharp teeth into the nearest finger.

"Run!" said Daniel and as the intruder paused instinctively to lick his wound, the two children were away, darting round the great heaps and back to the shelter of the familiar brickyard.

"I didn't like him," said Rosie disapprovingly as they sat panting in the shelter of the cowl again. "His finger tasted real horrid! Can I have another humbug to take the taste away?"

They sat in the warm, sucking contentedly, and Daniel wondered about the man. Clearly he was looking for something and had not wanted Batty Fred to see him there. He had come round to the back of the pile when he had seen the old man approaching and, stumbling upon the two children, had silenced them before they could speak and draw attention to his hiding place.

"Will he come after us?" asked Rosie.

Daniel shook his head. "Shouldn't think so. I reckon he was glad to see the back of us."

But what had the man been doing there? He was not a local man. Daniel suddenly remembered the stories the other boys had told him about London thieves who hid their loot in the rough stuff to get it out of the city. Once the police had searched a whole barge load at Otterham in search of stolen jewellery, but nothing had been found . . .

"Why won't he come after us?" Rosie seemed disappointed.

"Got something better to do than chase two kids."

"But what was he doing?"

"Dunno!" said Daniel, losing interest. "And what's more I don't care. We've got enough problems of our own without him, and now we've got to wait until he's gone before we can go on board the *Blackbird*."

"Never mind," said Rosie comfortingly. "We've still got six humbugs left and you can tell me that lovely story about the pirate with the wooden leg and the parrot and that story about climbing to the highest yard-arm in the awful storm and that one about . . ." Daniel sighed and launched into the time-honoured formula, "Once upon a time . . . "

As evening drew on and the light faded through the haze of rain, a small crack appeared in the lowering cloud and the sun showed through just above the horizon, red and gold and glaring like a round spy hole in a brick furnace. The sudden hot brilliance spilled out across the sky, filling the mists with a translucent orange glow and turning the dull grey clouds to shades of lavender and lilac. It flooded outward across the ruffled water transforming it into liquid gold and the moored boats became black silhouettes against the sudden glow. Daniel paused in his tale and the two children watched it wonderingly. Rosie found words for both of them.

"That," she said, "is real pretty."

Four stories later, and just as they reached the end of the humbugs, the man in the blue jacket finally abandoned his wet unappetizing search and set off for the more rewarding comforts of the Anchor and Hope. It was plain to see from the angry hunching of his shoulders and the hands thrust deep into empty pockets, that whatever he had been searching for, he had not found it.

"Now," said Daniel. They stretched cramped limbs, revived one of Rosie's feet which had gone to sleep, and crossed the open ground to the *Blackbird* as swiftly and unobtrusively as they could, though there was none to see them go. Daniel was a little concerned about how Joxer would react to Rosie's presence on board, but as he opened his mouth to bark officiously, Rosie flung her arms around his neck with the delighted cry of, "Oh, darling doggie!"

Daniel got a distinct impression that if a dog could have blushed, Joxer would have done so, but as it was he was reduced to standing helplessly as the waves of affection swept over him, wagging his tail a little nervously, while casting apologetic glances at Daniel.

"Why, Joxer, you're just an old softy," said Daniel. "And you're supposed to be a guard dog."

Rosie sprang to his defence. "I bet he's a very good guard dog", she said, "it's just that I have a way with dogs, Ma said so, and I always wanted one of my very own." The mention of her mother brought back the events of the day. "Oh, Daniel," she said, suddenly anxious again, "will Ma ever come back?"

"Of course she will," said Daniel with a confidence he was far from feeling. "She'll be back right as rain in a week or two."

"How will she know where I am? Did you leave a note?"

"Well I couldn't could I, stupid, or 'they' would have read it and come after you to take you to the orphanage. But we'll go up there every Sunday and see if she's back."

Rosie thought this was quite reasonable and turned her attention to her temporary home. While Daniel fixed them a hurried meal, she explored the barge with great enthusiasm and was torn between delight at the novelty of living on a boat and exclamations of dismay and disapproval when she surveyed its dingy cabins and leaky hull. For though a week of Daniel's efforts had removed much of the surface dirt from the *Blackbird*'s timbers and had plugged up some of the minor holes, it was clear that she was in an advanced stage of dilapidation.

The fo'c'sle, where Daniel lived, was small and cramped. A big locker for coal ran down either side with canvas pipecots above, and the old iron galley stove was set against the fore bulkhead. In the narrow forepeak were two large lockers used for storing the cloths which covered the decks and rigging during mud loading, and since it was Daniel's job to fetch these and store them away, he reckoned that it would be a safe place to hide Rosie when Batty Fred was around. Since he rarely set foot in the fo'c'sle but kept himself to himself in the more spacious Skipper's cabin at the far end of the barge, Daniel thought it would not be too difficult. After all, he thought, Batty Fred wasn't around all that much, except when they were under way, and then he was busy on deck. While they loaded mud he spent most of his time reading the papers in the muddies' privy, and when they were back at the quayside he was either drinking at the Anchor and Hope or sleeping off the after effects in his cabin.

Certainly there was no risk of his setting foot in the fo'c'sle that night so Daniel settled Rosie in the spare pipecot. The traumas of the day had tired her out and she was soon asleep, but Daniel's worries were not so easily put aside. He went up on deck, instinctively seeking solace in the wide quietness of his beloved river. The clouds still massed gun-metal grey overhead except where the dark blanket had slipped a little along the skyline. Here the wild glory of the setting sun had left behind a thin band of clear primrose which seemed to augur well for the coming day. The rain had stopped and the mist had cleared, and the water lay like glass across the estuary. The air smelt like clean washing hung out to dry. Daniel filled his lungs contentedly and turned to go below.

Eight

The *Blackbird* sailed for the mud hole very early the next morning. It was necessary that she should be there in time to start loading by seven o'clock, when the falling tide uncovered the top ledge of the mud hole. This gave the muddies four hours in which to load seventy-five tons of mud into the hold before the incoming tide covered the mud hole and refloated the barge again.

Batty Fred hated an early start on Monday morning even more that he did on any other morning. After a hard night spent drowning his sorrows in Dora's beer, he emerged red-eyed, unshaven and very bad tempered and proceeded to take it out on his defenceless crew.

Until then Daniel had been feeling quite pleased with himself. He had been up very early to wake Rosie and to rehearse with her the plans for keeping her out of Batty Fred's sight while giving her as much freedom as he could in the cramped quarters of the fo'c'sle. He had brewed tea and taken some to the old man at six as he had been instructed the night before, and then returned to make some stale bread into quite presentable dripping toast, a delicacy which soon came to the attention of Joxer's keen nose and brought him to join the feast.

Rosie was delighted with her new life. She had the young child's blessed ability to live for the present moment, untroubled by past and future, and unlike Daniel she managed for long periods to forget her anxiety for her mother in the excitement of her great adventure. It was true that she had shed a few tears when Daniel had put her to bed the night before, and had said a long chatty prayer for her mother's recovery and her father's safe return, but within minutes she had been asleep, thumb in mouth, rag doll against her cheek, while Daniel with all the foresight and responsibilities that came with being twelve years old, had lain awake half the night worrying. After breakfast he had bundled Rosie into the forepeak locker to separate her from Joxer, who seemed bent on spending the whole day being fussed and petted, and hauled the reluctant dog back on deck. The rain had stopped, though not for long thought Daniel; the promise of the previous evening had come to nothing for the western horizon was weighed down with a heavy mist of dark cloud. But the rising sun behind him filled the air between with brightness and lit up the seagulls so that they shone with an unnatural whiteness, soaring plaintively against the lowering sky. The air smelt sweet and salty, and in spite of all his problems, Daniel felt again the sense of joy and wonder which always filled him when he gazed out across the wide empty beauty of the marsh and the estuary. It didn't last long; it was almost immediately replaced by the sense of foreboding which came with the sight of Batty Fred's bloodshot eyes emerging from the after-cabin scuttle hatch.

"Am I paying you to admire the view, you young skiver?" he shouted, as he climbed up on deck. "We've a day's work to be done, and a barge to get under way."

"Yes, Mr Batey." Daniel leapt to the tasks which were more pleasure than work to him, and thrilled as the *Blackbird* moved away from the mud wharf and heeled a little to the power of the wind.

Batty Fred kept him busy with a succession of fiddling jobs and when he ran out of these, told him to fetch the boat hook and haul aboard some of the driftwood that floated by, to be dried and burned in the galley stove. This was a tricky operation and more than once Daniel came close to toppling over the side as he lunged at a drifting log, only to have it bob out of reach as the *Blackbird*'s bow wave caught it.

Then, as he prepared to take aim at a whole raft of bobbing planks, feeling reasonably sure of hitting one of them, he noticed an odd little metal tube that projected above the water close by. It turned over at the top and ended in a round circle which faced towards him. As he watched, it seemed to turn away and then vanished suddenly beneath the waves. He blinked in surprise, and puzzled a little over what it might have been, but it did not re-appear and he decided that it was probably only a piece of submerged wreckage. He turned his mind back to his salvage operation and had managed to haul a substantial pile of driftwood on board by the time they reached the mud hole.

The wind had carried off the clouds and the warm sun was shining by the time the muddies got on board and the leather-hinged doors of the muddies' boat privy had swung shut behind Batty Fred.

Daniel, tying the last of the mud cloths into place and welcoming the burly gang like old friends, wished he could call Rosie up on deck to join in the fun. Joxer, whining at the fo'c'sle hatch, seemed to have much the same idea.

"What's up with him?" asked the ganger. "You got something tasty hidden away down there, young Daniel?"

Joxer scrabbled his paws against the hatch-cover and Daniel said hastily, "It was a rat. He caught a rat yesterday . . . I expect he's after another."

"You should let him down there then see if he can catch them. Nasty things, rats."

"Oh, well . . . " Daniel thought quickly. "They go under the floorboards . . . he can't get at them but he scratches the paintwork. I'd better not let him. Joxer, do come away!"

Joxer gave a short sharp bark to show his contempt for this tall story and then went on whining. Daniel prayed that Rosie would not decide to let him in. But once the work was under way and the air was full of flying mud, Joxer decided that discretion was the better part of valour, and went off to investigate the wonderful salty and fishy smells of the marshes.

Daniel finished his chores, and checked to see if Rosie was all right. She wasn't: she was bored and irritable and cross that he would not stay down in the forepeak and keep her company.

"I can't, not for too long," Daniel told her. "It would look too suspicious. I'll have to go up on deck again." He hunted around, found a pencil stub and an old piece of brown wrapping paper and left her drawing a picture.

Ten minutes later he was sitting in the sun on the fo'c'sle scuttle, trying to clean up the starboard lamp, when without warning a wall of moving air struck him like a great invisible hand, pushing him backwards and carrying away the cloth from his hand. It was followed a split second later by a thunderous roar of sound, then something fast and heavy came out of the blue void of the sky with a whistling shriek and, missing him by a hair's breadth, crashed through the thick deck timber down into the fo'c'sle below.

For a moment, Daniel was too astonished to be frightened, but when he saw the hole in the deck and realized that Rosie was below, he was suddenly sick with apprehension. He shouted, "Rosie!" and as if in answer to his cry there came from below a great shriek of fright and rage. Daniel dived down the scuttle hatch to see if she was injured, praying as he went that fate would spare him this last terrible blow.

Now at this point, with Rosie's screams rising loud and clear on the summer air, her presence on board would immediately have become known to all the muddies alongside, had it not been for an even more compelling circumstance that had directed their attention elsewhere, and given rise to such a loud bellowing of laughter among them that even Rosie's screams passed unheard.

For the mysterious explosion which had so rudely shattered the peace of the saltings had blown the upturned boat of the muddies' privy flat on its back, and Batty Fred lay trapped within it like an overturned tortoise in its shell, his legs waving pathetically from the sawn-off end.

It was almost too much for the muddies to bear. They

lent on their wooden spades laughing until tears of joy ran down their faces, and it was some time before they could walk steadily enough to go to the old man's assistance. And when at last they did stumble off in his direction, supporting each other as they went, it was in truth as much to get a closer view of the spectacle as to rescue Batty Fred from his unseemly predicament.

Back in the fo'c'sle cabin, Daniel knelt on the floor holding a tearful and badly frightened Rosie tightly in his arms and rocking her gently as he tried to soothe her panic.

"It's all right, it's all over," he told her, hoping against hope that it was. "There must have been an explosion somewhere and something has hit the *Blackbird*. But you're not hurt are you?"

Rosie shook her head. The crying died to an occasional heavy sniff, and after he had found her handkerchief and wiped her eyes, Daniel said, "Come on now, one big blow and then we'll look out and see what the damage is."

Rosie snorted like a grampus, and he protested, "Don't blow a hole through the handkerchief, young Rosie!" This made her laugh, as indeed it was intended to, and Daniel soon diverted her attention to the search for the offending missile.

It turned out to be a sizeable piece of mis-shapen metal which had torn a hole through the deck, knocked a chunk from one corner of the cast-iron galley stove and finally buried itself in the thick timber of the bulkhead.

"Something's blown up in the Dockyard, I shouldn't wonder," said Daniel, feeling suddenly that the war was not just something men went off to fight, but something that might come and find you wherever you were.

As he was trying unsuccessfully to prise the metal

lump from the timber with an old kitchen knife, he suddenly realized how quiet it was and that in spite of Rosie's screams, no one had come to investigate her presence.

He popped his head out of the scuttle and found that the muddies had gone. Emerging farther he found that they were gathered in a small group in the distance and that they seemed to be finding something very entertaining. It took him a moment or two to realize what had happened, and then he began to laugh too.

"What is it?" asked Rosie, popping her head out beside him.

"It's Batty Fred, he's stuck in the privy and the blast has blown it over. Look, you can see his feet waving out of one end."

"That's rude!" said Rosie primly, and then as her sense of humour got the upper hand she added, "Rude . . . but very funny!" and she began to giggle.

The force that had laid Batty Fred flat, had also blown the two doors inward and jammed them shut. But the muddies, reluctant to part with such a good joke a moment too soon, simply picked up the whole half-boat and carried it back to the *Blackbird* with Batty Fred's angry boots still protruding.

"Put your head down, Rosie, before someone looks up and sees you."

Reluctantly she climbed back down to the fo'c'sle. "I shall miss the fun," she complained.

"Well, there won't be much fun when Batty Fred gets out. He'll be hopping mad; especially when he sees the hole in the deck. If he finds you here too, we'll really be in trouble." And in spite of her protest he bundled her back into the forepeak locker in case the old man should come below.

Then, feeling that a mug of tea might help a little to soothe Batty Fred's ruffled feelings, he put the kettle on to boil.

When the muddies finally prised open the doors with their wooden fly tools and released the disgruntled old man, he stamped away angrily down into the after-cabin with a face like thunder. Daniel took him a cup of tea, but his offering met with such a hostile reception that he left it outside and withdrew hastily.

"Got a mug for us then, young Danny?" asked the ganger.

Daniel made a face at him. "I would if I could," he hissed, "but I think it would be the last straw for Batty Fred!"

The ganger gave him a broad wink. "That's all right, son," he said, "you're a good lad."

And wiping the last tears of laughter from their eyes the muddies picked up their fly tools and returned to their loading. For the tide was making and would not wait whatever the hazards of the day.

By the time the *Blackbird* was fully loaded, the clouds were massing and the rain began again, a light but steady drizzle spreading across the estuary. It seemed a fitting background for Batty Fred when at last he emerged on to the deck. Daniel had expected a towering rage and was surprised at first to find him in a state of mournful gloom, but passing close by him he caught a strong whiff of alcohol and realized why his mug of tea had cooled unheeded outside the after-cabin door. Fortunately, the old man could sail the barge as well drunk as he could sober and, on the whole, Daniel preferred his maudlin mood to his usual bad temper.

The wind which had brought the rain carried them out of the mud hole without too much trouble and they were soon clear of the creek and fetched up into Saltpan Reach.

Batty Fred had not yet found out about the hole in the forepeak deck. Daniel was waiting for a suitable moment to break the news to him and in the meantime he had covered it with a pile of folded mud cloths. Of course, there was no way in which he could be personally blamed for the damage, but Daniel felt sure that when Batty Fred saw it, he would vent his anger on the only person within reach.

Then as they came along towards Kethole Reach another barge passed them going the other way and the mate, anxious to pass on a piece of extraordinary news, shouted across to Daniel:

"You 'eard the news? Them rotten 'Uns sank the *Bulldog* right here in Kethole."

"But how?" Daniel found it impossible to believe that any harm could have come to one of those towering battleships in the shelter of the Medway, surrounded by the might of England's navy.

"That ruddy submarine, of course! Stands to reason. That's why the rest of 'em have put out their torpedo netting." He waved a hand towards the remainder of the fleet.

The two barges were rapidly passing out of ear-shot but the voice came drifting back across the water.

"One of the rescue boats saw a periscope . . . sticking up out of the water . . . "

As the voice was lost on the wind, Daniel had a sudden memory of the odd little metal tube which had vanished

95

without warning earlier in the day. Had he imagined it? Had it in fact been no more than a piece of wreckage? Or was there really an enemy at large in the grey waters beneath them?

He raised his eyes from the oily swell to stare incredulously at the gap in the great line of grey warships which was all that remained to show where the towering shape of the *Bulldog* had been. In the gap a flurry of small naval craft were vainly scouring the scanty wreckage for any traces of survivors, or for any clues as to how the disaster had come about. A patrol boat circled the area keeping the passing river traffic at bay and forcing the *Blackbird* to tack short of her usual mark.

Rather to Daniel's surprise, the sinking of the *Bulldog* seemed to arouse a strong patriotic fervour in Batty Fred. His alcoholic gloom deepened as he contemplated the fate of the great warship and his hostility towards "them fiendish Huns" knew no bounds, especially since he now saw them as the perpetrators of the explosion which had subjected him to such indignity earlier in the day. At last Daniel judged it safe to draw his attention to the hole in the foredeck, since he must needs be told sooner or later and at the moment his anger was more likely to be vented against the Kaiser than to descend on Daniel's head.

He took the last of the mud cloths down below and made sure that Rosie was well hidden in the forepeak locker before announcing as if he had just discovered it:

"Mr Batey look here! See what those rotten Huns have done to the *Blackbird*; there's a hole right through the deck!"

Batty Fred swore horribly and called Daniel to take the wheel and hold the barge steady while he went for'ard.

Surveying the damage, he seemed torn between rage against the Germans and a strange excitement at finding his boat a direct victim of enemy action. It was as if this personal involvement in the explosion which had destroyed the great *Bulldog*, gave him a proprietary interest in the incident. Daniel could see that it would prove a useful tale for gaining Dora's attention and sympathy at the Anchor and Hope. Moreover, by enabling the old man to appear in a heroic light — "Thames Barge comes under Enemy Fire, Narrow Escape for Skipper Fred Batey" — it would help to counter the ludicrous tale which the muddies had to tell.

When he had finished swearing at the damage on deck, Batty Fred disappeared down the fo'c'sle hatchway in search of further evidence of the Kaiser's infamy, re-emerging only briefly to shout to Daniel, "Keep one eye on that bob up there, lad, and if you let her gybe I'll skin you alive!"

In the silence that followed, Daniel mentally crossed his fingers and hoped that Rosie would not move. But to his dismay Joxer, who had been sitting quietly at his feet, jumped up as Batty Fred slid back the fo'c'sle hatch and hurried for'ard in search of Rosie, who for some reason beyond the dog's comprehension seemed to be playing hide and seek.

"Joxer! come back!" Daniel's cry was low but urgent. The dog took no notice but vanished down the hatch after Batty Fred. With the *Blackbird* under way and the wind freshening there was no way Daniel could leave the wheel to go after him, and indeed in any other circumstance he would not have wished to. Holding the wheel steady as the boat surged forward, her bows carving a pathway through the water and her masts seeming to sweep the scudding clouds above him: this had been his dream ever since he had first fallen in love with the Thames barges. The wind filled the dark sails in a tight straining curve, the rigging sang and he could feel the gentle surge of the deck beneath his feet. But as a dream without warning can turn a corner into nightmare, so Daniel waited for some sound that would mean that Rosie had been discovered and that his hard-won sailing life was at an end. Joxer would go straight to Rosie's hiding place, of that he felt sure. And if Batty Fred, suspecting a rat, opened the locker door and let him in . . . well, no one, least of all a little girl of Rosie's age, could stay quiet under the impetus of Joxer's friendly greeting. And yet no sound came from the direction of the forepeak and as the minutes passed Batty Fred did not re-emerge.

Daniel waited and wondered and at last even began to hope that some providence was on his side and that after all Rosie had not been discovered. But there he was wrong — wrong at least in his hope that Rosie was undiscovered but not, perhaps, in his belief that some providence was at work. For though afterwards it was always a source of regret to Daniel that he had missed that first encounter which was to open up a completely new chapter in Batty Fred's life, yet if he had been present at the time, things would almost certainly have turned out very differently.

When Batty Fred, who was, to use an appropriate nautical expression, "three sheets in the wind", staggered mournfully down the fo'c'sle steps to see what damage the *Blackbird* had sustained, he was already suffering from an advanced attack of alcohol-induced self-pity. It had started at the Anchor and Hope the night before when Dora had paid him less attention than usual, she being distracted not only by the hated Punchy and his cronies, but also by the presence of a stranger at the bar. He had blown in wet and surly halfway through the evening and ordered a large brandy to drive out the cold. Dora, in her role as landlady and hostess, had naturally felt obliged to chat to him and put him at his ease — she might even have been a little intrigued by the large roll of white bank notes which he had flashed around while paying for his drink. Under the influence of her attention and the tongue-loosening brandy, he had lost his surly air and become noisy and boastful with the self-confident swagger of a London bully among lesser provincial mortals. He had hinted at his connection with powerful men in the city's underworld and Dora, for whom new faces were few and far between, had listened enthralled, leaning across the bar with her chin propped up on one white arm muttering, "Would you credit it?" and "Oh, my word!" during appropriate pauses.

When Fred, whose mug had been empty for too long, intervened with a sarcastic dig at the bad service, the stranger had barely deigned to notice him and had ordered Dora to, "Fill up the old fool's mug, my love," as if he owned the place. Only the fear that the man might indeed have powerful criminal connections had kept Batty Fred from quarrelling openly with him, but in the event he had been forced to content himself with seething resentfully in his corner and drinking himself into a state of gloom and despondency.

He had been only half-way through sleeping it off next morning when Daniel had woken him as instructed for an early start to the mud hole. The incident when the muddies' privy had been blown over had done nothing to restore his good humour, indeed it had sent him straight back to the bottle to blot out the memory of the muddies' laughter, which still rang in his ears.

And now as if a malign fate could never tire of heaping insults upon him, the hated Kaiser had singled out the *Blackbird* for a personal attack, carving a hole through her deck, tearing a lump out of her galley stove and leaving a jagged lump of shrapnel embedded in her bulkhead.

"Poor old *Blackbird*," he muttered thickly. "Only friend I've got . . .", and feeling the need to remove the offending missile from her open wound he took down an old kitchen knife from the galley rack and began prodding at the misshapen metal. But his hand was as unsteady as his feet and as he leant his full weight on the knife handle the blade snapped suddenly, throwing him off balance so that he lurched sideways, tripped over Joxer – who for some inexplicable reason was scrabbling at the door of the forepeak locker – and ended up in a heap on the floor clutching a bleeding hand where the broken blade had caught it.

It was the last straw: the camel's back gave way under the load. Batty Fred sat in the middle of the fo'c'sle floor and lost the will to live.

"I shall sit here until I bleed to death," he announced reproachfully to whatever gods there might be who had chosen to make such malevolent sport of him. "I shall just bleed slowly to death and no one will care . . . what am I anyway? Just a laughing stock for those mud-caked loonies . . . the Kaiser is out to get me . . . Dora doesn't love me any more . . . and I don't have a friend in the world," and he began to weep maudlin, fifty-per-cent alcohol tears.

And then, "Nonsense!" said a small, firm, feminine voice.

Batty Fred's sunken head jerked suddenly upright. He stared around him.

"Dora?" he said incredulously. "Is that you?" And when no answer came he shook his head as if to clear it and muttered, "Must be going round the bend . . . could have swore I heard a voice say, 'Nonsense'."

"Yes, you did," said the voice again. "Of course it's nonsense. You can't just sit and bleed to death. For one thing it would make the most awful mess all over the floor."

"Dora?" said Batty Fred again, staring around him unable to believe that divine voices could take any other form.

But at that moment Joxer's wild scrabbling finally proved too much for the old catch on the locker door; it gave way, and the door swung slowly open to reveal Rosie sitting calmly on top of the pile of folded mud cloths.

"No," she said, "not Dora: my name is Rosie."

Batty Fred who wasn't seeing things at all clearly, shook his head until the two images merged into one. It was always dim in the fo'c'sle and in the locker it was even darker. He peered into its shadow.

"Rosie?" he asked, bewildered by this odd turn of events but far enough gone to accept anything. "Who's Rosie?"

And then Rosie, who had been touched by his sad claim to be without a friend in the world, said exactly the right thing.

"I," she told him firmly, "am your friend; and what's more," she added, "I'm going to tie up your poor hand, so that you won't bleed to death all over the floor."

She enjoyed repeating the spine-tingling phrase "bleed to death", and she had decided to minister to his injured hand, not for any altruistic reason, but because she had always wanted to tear her petticoat up in strips to make a bandage, as heroines did in stories, and for once her mother was not around to spank her for doing it.

So while Batty Fred sat on the floor bemused and unquestioning, she ripped and tore to her heart's content and bound up his cut (which would quite adequately have been covered by a small square of sticking plaster), until his entire hand had disappeared like some hibernating insect into a large, untidy, white cocoon.

"There," she said sitting back and surveying the result, "I should think that would do."

While she had been working, Batty Fred had been searching his puzzled brain for some explanation of how she had got there. It seemed an impertinent question to ask of a ministering angel, and he was still trying to pluck up courage to broach the subject when the *Blackbird* gave a sudden lurch and he became aware of Daniel's voice calling his name from some immeasurable distance away.

Batty Fred scrambled to his feet. "Stay there!" he instructed Rosie firmly, wagging a finger at her, "and *don't* go away." For he strongly suspected that she was a figment of his alcoholic imagination and was very much afraid that she would disappear if he took his eyes off her.

"Don't worry," said Rosie serenely, "I shan't."

But he was not convinced and went backwards up the steps, watching her until the last moment in case her image should waver and vanish before his eyes.

Up on deck, Daniel had been calling him frantically for some minutes, knowing that it was high time to put the barge about if they were to make Lower Field Creek.

Drunk or sober, Batty Fred was first and always a sailorman and he took the wheel in a moment.

Daniel stared at the bandaged hand and racked his memory to recall where he had seen the material before. Batty Fred caught him staring and shouted, "Well, don't stand about gawping. Stand by to brail in the main, and jump to it, lad."

For the next ten minutes the *Blackbird* was a flurry of activity and then they were alongside the mud wharf and it was time to prepare for unloading.

"I'll get the mud cloths," said Daniel quickly, anxious to see how Rosie was surviving in the dark cupboard.

"No!" said Batty Fred quickly, "I'll fetch 'em."

Daniel was aghast, having no idea of the scene which had already taken place in the fo'c'sle. He bit his lip and stared helplessly at Batty Fred's retreating back. Then, as the old man disappeared down the companionway, he had a sudden picture of Rosie's distress when the locker was opened and her hiding place revealed. He decided that instant confession was the only way to divert Batty Fred's wrath on to his own head, and he ran after him shouting, "Mr Batey, there is something I have to tell you . . . "

But when he had clambered down the steps, he found Rosie laying out mugs and spoons and the old tin kettle humming on the galley stove.

"I thought you'd both like a nice cup of tea, my dears," said Rosie, who had tired of playing "nurses" and was now playing "mothers".

Both equally baffled, Daniel and Batty Fred sat down side by side on the starboard bunk, each facing straight ahead but with eyes that flicked sideways to catch the other's reaction to Rosie's unexpected presence.

Rosie turned round and seeing their obvious discomfiture beamed sweetly at both of them.

"Have you two met?" she asked innocently, and then in her best party manner, "Daniel, this is my friend, Mr Batey; Mr Batey, this is my brother Daniel."

"We've met," said Batty Fred briefly. He scowled crossly at Daniel, who seemed suddenly to have acquired some kind of relationship with his own newly found friend and ministering angel.

Daniel was quite simply lost for words. As the two of them sat watching Rosie spooning tea from the battered old tea caddy into the cracked teapot, he was aware that the old man had already met her and that for some reason he accepted her presence on board. But why, when he seemed to be at odds with all the world, he should make an exception for Rosie, was beyond Daniel's understanding.

But the truth was that while Batty Fred considered all men to be better or worse versions of Punchy Kitson, unscrupulous enemies and rivals for Dora's affection, and all boys to be unprincipled little scoundrels who would in their turn grow up to be more Punchy Kitsons; nevertheless, he actually liked little girls. By the same simple logic he saw them as miniatures of Dora: kind, sympathetic creatures, whose only fault lay in a tendency to be led astray by the Punchy Kitsons of this world. Indeed the only other person besides Dora for whom Batty Fred had previously cherished any affection was his niece Annie, and he had only sent her into service after her father's death to get her away from the evil influence of Jem Kitson, who had of course committed the unforgivable sin of being Punchy Kitson's son.

So his principal reaction when Rosie appeared mysteriously from the dark recesses of his fo'c'sle locker to bandage his wounds, comfort his sorrows, and brew him a nice hot cup of tea, was a strange, incredulous delight. It was only slightly dimmed by the discovery that Daniel, from whom he would have been only too ready to protect her, seemed to be claiming some kind of proprietorial interest.

As the kettle came to the boil, both man and boy jumped up with cries of, "I'll see to that, you might scald yourself . . . " and then stood glaring at each other, while the kettle boiled all over the stove.

Rosie took charge. "Would you do it, please, Mr Batey," she said tactfully.

Batty Fred flashed Daniel a look of triumph and poured the boiling water on to the tea, somehow managing to scald his good hand in the hot steam as he did so. Rosie offered to bandage it with what remained of her petticoat but, realizing that another of her bandages would completely incapacitate him, he assured her that it would do with a bit of butter rubbed on it.

"Butter is bad for burns," said Rosie. "Ma says so. You'd better put it in some cold water, and then Daniel will tell you my sad, sad story."

With one hand in a cocoon of bandage and the other in a bucket of cold water, Batty Fred was soon quite helpless; so that Rosie had to hold his mug of tea for him to sip while Daniel told the story of his father's absence at the war, his mother's sudden illness, and his desperate decision to hide his sister on board the *Blackbird*. Whenever Fred tried to speak, Rosie gave him another sip of tea, so Daniel was able to tell his story with maximum effect, painting a fearsome picture of the innocent Rosie threatened with imprisonment in some far-off orphanage.

When he finished, Rosie said, "But it's all right now, Danny, because Mr Batey is my friend and he would never let them take me away. Would you, Mr Batey?" and as Batty Fred opened his mouth to answer, she poured in some more tea and added, "There, you see Daniel. I told you he would let me stay."

But when the mug was empty and Batty Fred finally managed to get a word out, it seemed that Rosie was quite right. It was agreed between them that no one else should know of her presence on board the *Blackbird* and that she must stay below deck whenever they were alongside in case the powers-that-be should come looking for her, but apart from that she was to have the freedom of the barge.

"However did you do it?" Daniel asked her later that day, when they were alone together.

"Oh, I just have a way with people," said Rosie airily, "same as I do with dogs."

And with that Daniel had to be content.

Nine

The shock of the *Bulldog*'s disaster was somewhat overshadowed in the office of the Lower Field Brickworks by a closer and more immediate crisis. Someone at sometime had, it seemed, mislaid an order, and a message had arrived from an irate customer complaining that his building job would soon come to a halt for want of bricks. The customer, who was a good one, had been assured by Mr Jarvis that the bricks would be unloaded at Chelsea Wharf for him to collect within twenty-four hours. The *Windhawk* had been expected back on the tide, and it would have been possible to divert her for this short trip up river. But within half an hour a telegram had arrived from Punchy Kitson warning that the *Windhawk* would be delayed at Putney by a small but essential running repair, and Mr Jarvis found himself in an awkward situation, with plenty of bricks and a customer who wanted them at once if not sooner, and no way of delivering them. He sat with the offending telegram in his hands staring out gloomily at the wharfside, empty except for the decrepit silhouette of the *Blackbird*, which had just moored up at the mud wharf.

It was in fact, at this very moment, down in the fo'c'sle that Batty Fred sat helpless with one hand bandaged and the other in a bucket of water, while Rosie kept him quiet with sips of tea and Daniel told the sad story of her rescue from the clutches of the orphanage authorities. If Mr Jarvis had chosen that moment to go aboard her, things might have turned out quite differently, but as it was the idea of sending the *Blackbird* up river with a load of bricks was not one that leapt readily to mind. For one thing it was not the Company's policy to give brick freights to the few independent Skippers: these profitable trips were reserved for the Company's own barges. And for another thing, Mr Jarvis hardly saw the *Blackbird* as a sailing barge. She was so run down and patched up that he thought of her, if he thought of her at all, as a floating mud bucket. But circumstances alter cases and after he had sat for half an hour calculating the relative positions of his entire fleet of barges, and reluctantly coming to the conclusion that none could be contacted or diverted in time, he slowly began to perceive the *Blackbird*'s stumpy rig, with its sails untidily brailed like some old badly folded umbrella, as a possible way out of his problem. It took him several hours longer, however, to reach a decision, since it went against the grain to consign a load of his precious new bricks to such an unworthy container. But it came to him at last that he might use her to dispatch a small advance consignment of ten thousand bricks to keep the letter of his promise, and follow up with the other thirty thousand in the *Windhawk* as soon as she returned.

Once he had made up his mind, he went down to the mud wharf just as the unloading was completed, and was slightly reassured by the sight of Daniel Swann on the *Blackbird*'s after deck, removing the mud cloths from around her main horse and scraping off the heavy clay with meticulous care.

"How do you like the sailing life, then?" he called to the lad, and was rewarded by a startled glance followed by a smile of recognition, and then, as he absorbed and considered the unexpected question, a look of pure joy.

"Oh, it's marvellous, Mr Jarvis! It's just what I always wanted."

The brickyard manager raised his eyebrows in a gesture of mild astonishment and not liking to ask, "How are you getting on with that disagreeable old curmudgeon Fred Batey?", he inquired cautiously, "Is Mr Batey pleased with you, then?"

Again to his astonishment the boy's face broke into a smile.

"Oh, yes . . . at least I think so. He has been *very* kind to me."

It was not true, of course, but Daniel was still bathed in a rosy glow of gratitude over Batty Fred's decision to let Rosie stay on board, and this one kindly act in his moment of greatest need, had quite wiped out of his memory the long tally of the old man's meannesses.

"Well, then," said Mr Jarvis when he had recovered from his astonishment, "I'm very pleased to hear it. Eh, perhaps I might come below and have a word with him."

"No . . . " said Daniel hastily, for Batty Fred, still immobilized on Rosie's orders, was watching her peel potatoes in the fo'c'sle galley. "That is . . . I mean, yes, of course . . . but you don't need to come on board, it's still a bit muddy . . . I'll ask him to come up."

When the old man emerged on deck, Mr Jarvis was concerned to find that his left hand was heavily bandaged.

"Is that serious?" he asked.

Batty Fred frowned doubtfully at the cocoon around his left hand and tried to remember what lay inside it.

"No . . . just a cut . . . " he said at last. "Deep though . . . bled quite a lot. Should 'ave stopped by now."

As he spoke a strong whiff of cheap brandy assailed Mr Jarvis's teetotal nostrils and he paused, wondering if he was doing the right thing. He spoke firmly, "Look, Batey, I have an order needs delivering in a hurry and the *Windhawk* is delayed. If you can scrub out your hold and sober up within a couple of hours, I'll give you a freight of bricks to take up to Chelsea."

Batty Fred stared at him stupidly as if unable to make sense of what he had said, but Daniel was beside himself with joy.

"Oh, yes, Mr Jarvis!" he said "I can get it all scrubbed out, I promise you, and Mr Batey has already had three cups of tea; by the time he's had supper, he'll be fine."

"What do you say, Batey?" Mr Jarvis frowned and fixed Batty Fred's bloodshot eyes with his most authoritative stare.

Batty Fred, who felt that between Daniel and Rosie he was beginning to have very little say in the running of the *Blackbird*, nodded obediently and, touching his fore-finger to his battered bowler hat, said, "Right you are, Mr Jarvis, sir. We'll have her ready first thing tomorrow morning."

"No, she'll have to be ready in a couple of hours, Batey.

These bricks have to be in Chelsea by early afternoon tomorrow, otherwise I shouldn't be offering you the freight in the first place."

Batty Fred shook his head. "*Blackbird* would never make it," he said pessimistically.

Mr Jarvis ignored his comment. "I want her loaded by eight o'clock this evening," he said firmly. "You can get out on the last of the ebb and take the first of the flood up the London river. You've a good wind: should make Woolwich before it slackens and I'll have a tug standing by to take you on from there."

"She'll be ready, I promise," said Daniel, and with that, since for all his youth Daniel Swann seemed the more reliable of the two, Mr Jarvis had to be content.

And so it was that Batty Fred, who, since the first light that morning, had been personally attacked by the Kaiser, humiliated by the muddies, and bandaged into a state of incapacity by Rosie, now found that the management of his affairs seemed to have passed into Daniel's hands. He decided wisely to retire to his own cabin and sleep it off.

Daniel and Rosie had a marvellous time cleaning the hold, a task that involved a lot of scrubbing with old brooms and the throwing about of bucket after bucket of salty water. Rosie tucked her skirts into her knickers and splashed around in the shallow water inside the hold and said "it was better than a day at Margate".

By late afternoon the *Blackbird's* hold was clean enough to satisfy Mr Jarvis's eagle eye and two hours later the freight of bricks had been loaded aboard. The sight of their neat, glowing red stacks filled Daniel's heart with joy, and as he contemplated the voyage ahead of them, he began to feel that his reluctant apprenticeship was rapidly turning into the kind of sailing life he had always planned for himself. Even Batty Fred, once he had sobered up, seemed to relish this unexpected return to a life more varied and dignified than the mud work. Daniel would have been surprised if he could have known how much this change in the old man's outlook sprang from Rosie's presence on board. She was to be the audience for whom he would replay his former role of skilful and respected sailing-barge Skipper.

They were away by eight o'clock, slipping down the Medway on the last of the ebb tide, to wait off Grain Edge for the rising flood. They found many more sailing barges there, waiting for the same tide: some had come down from the east-coast ports; others around the Kent coast from the south coast of England or the northern ports of France; and all were bound for the busy, crowded, narrowing stream of the London river. The light was fading now and Daniel's first thought was that he was glad of it. In the dusk the *Blackbird* became just one of the many anonymous waiting vessels, her decrepitude masked by the coming night. But once they were under way he began to have his doubts about the advantages of making the passage by night. Moving upstream among the melée of tacking barges, soon visible only as shadowy black forms under warning lights, he began to have serious doubts about Batty Fred's ability to deal with this complex challenge. For besides the sailing barges there were many other craft in the river, tugs pulling strings of dumb barges, ocean-going sailing ships under tow, and incoming steamers bound for the London docks. The late-night ferries crossed the river from side to side and outgoing steamers came down river riding against the flood. But Daniel found that Batty Fred seemed to call up a long lifetime's knowledge of the Thames from somewhere inside his addled brain, and had moved back in time to rediscover the lost skills of his prime.

Rosie loved every minute of it: watching the ever-changing pattern of lights and relishing the thrill as each set of warning lights grew relentlessly closer and closer, only to pass ahead or astern at the last possible moment. And when, after one particularly close shave, she clapped her hands ecstatically and exclaimed, "Oh Mr Batey, you must be the cleverest sailor on the whole river!", Batty Fred felt a glow of pride and satisfaction so foreign to his recent experience that he hardly recognized it for what it was, and told himself crossly that he was going soft in his old age.

At last Rosie fell asleep on deck, tired out by the fresh air and the excitement of the day, and Batty Fred entrusted the wheel to Daniel for a few glorious moments while he carried her down below and tucked her up in her bunk.

She was woken again by the tooting of the officious little tug which met them at Woolwich as the tide slackened and, throwing them a tow rope, hauled them steadily on upstream against the growing strength of the ebb.

Below Tower Bridge they moored up while the *Blackbird*'s mast and spars were lowered to the deck to enable them to pass under the numerous bridges which lay between them and their destination. Daniel found this operation rather an alarming one since the *Blackbird*'s rigging was never in first-class condition. He made certain that Rosie stood well out of the way as the stayfall lowered the massive spars flat along the deck with all their sails and rigging jumbled about them, and he breathed a sigh of relief when all was safely stowed and they were under way again.

Rosie made them some delicious, if somewhat lopsided, cheese and chutney sandwiches for breakfast, which they ate sitting in the sunshine on the hatch-cover and watching the landmarks of London glide by. She then decided that it would be appropriate for them to sing sea shanties as they went along. To Daniel's astonishment Batty Fred joined in with a voice like a rusty hinge, and they reached Chelsea at last to the not inappropriate strains of "What Shall We Do with the Drunken Sailor".

Ten

Earlier the same morning, the news of the sinking of the *Bulldog* hung over Alfred Fanshaw's breakfast table at Number 17 Tadema Terrace like a grey pall. Lily Tompkins was triumphant, as he had known she would be.

" . . . well, it stands to reason," she was saying excitedly for the umpteenth time, "that if those in authority listened to them as works on the river and lives by it, they'd have known all about that there submarine what blowed it up. And Cook says . . . " She paused for breath, and before Beatrice could say wearily, "Yes, thank you Lily, that will *do*," Alfred leapt recklessly into the argument.

"There is absolutely no truth in the story about a submarine in the river," he announced in his official Admiralty spokesman voice. "Though the Admiralty are deeply concerned about the loss of this great battleship, and though the official inquiry into the incident has yet to take place, it seems probable that the explosion was caused accidentally while loading ammunition . . . "

"You just read that in *The Times*," said Lily scornfully. "I know because Cook read it out to us before breakfast and she says you can't believe nothing you read in the papers."

"As it happens," said Alfred pompously, "I was the one who drafted that statement to be sent to *The Times* and I should know whether . . . " A thought struck him. "And what was Cook doing reading my *Times* anyway? You know perfectly well that no one is allowed to open my newspaper. I can't bear a crumpled newspaper . . . "

"Oh, it's all right," said Lily cheerfully. "We always keep a flat iron on the stove and I give it a quick run over when we've all finished with it, just to make the creases nice."

"That's not the point," said Alfred crossly. "I am the Master of this household and I am entitled to know the news first."

"Well in that case," said Lily pertly, "you'll have to get up earlier and talk to the milkman's boy. He always knows everything before *The Times* does."

"Thank you, Lily," said Beatrice firmly, since Alfred seemed temporarily bereft of words and was slowly turning purple. "That will be all, Lily."

When the door had closed behind the maid, Beatrice said, "You really shouldn't argue with her, Alfred. It only encourages her."

"She'll have to go!" said Alfred in a strangled voice, when he could speak again.

"That's easy for you to say, but with half the young women working in the munitions factories, it's not easy to find housemaids."

"Why can't Annie serve breakfast then?"

"Because she has to take the children out immediately afterwards and she is busy having her own meal."

"She could have it first."

"She's busy laying our table."

"Lily can do that."

"Lily is helping Cook . . . oh really, Alfred, you must allow me to supervise my own domestic staff."

"Well, I shall speak to Cook severely, she has no business to read my paper!"

"Oh Alfred, not today!" Beatrice was in despair. "I have a luncheon for the Ladies' Guild to discuss ways of raising money for the comforts for the troops and Lady Crumleigh is coming. If you upset Cook, she'll give notice and the luncheon will be a disaster. Oh, my goodness, just look at the time!" And she did her best to speed her husband on his way to the Admiralty, where she felt that his interference would be less dangerous than it was at home. She had been working and planning for today's luncheon party for weeks and was in a nervous flutter for fear something should go wrong. At least, Charles and Elinor were behaving themselves today, she thought, smiling fondly at their two heads demurely bent over the porridge bowls.

In fact, Charlie was trying unsuccessfully to feed porridge lumps to a white mouse which was sitting on his lap. He had acquired it from the butcher's boy as a swap for his penknife but had forgotten to find out what it ate. Nora leaned across surreptitiously and sprinkled a pinch of sugar on the porridge lumps but the mouse remained unconvinced.

"Yes, high time I was on my way."

Alfred rose to his feet suddenly with a sharp scrape of his chair against the polished linoleum of the floor, startling the mouse, which jumped from Charlie's grasp in a flash. It sped across the floor, unnoticed by Alfred or Beatrice, and vanished into one of the hollow ends of the bamboo framework of Beatrice's highly fashionable Chinese cabinet.

"Now, children," said Beatrice, "time to get ready for your walk."

"Oh, can't we stay and clear away the breakfast things to help you, since everyone is so busy preparing for the luncheon?"

Elinor's face was a picture of willing innocence and Beatrice brightened. Could it be, she thought, that her long struggle to civilize her unruly offspring was at last having some effect.

"What a kind thought . . . but just stack the plates dear. Leave Lily to carry the tray downstairs." She knew how often and how easily their good intentions ended in disaster.

As soon as she was out of the room, Charlie and Nora flew to the Chinese cabinet and pushed and shoved as each tried to get an eye to the hole in the end of the bamboo. The hole should not have been there at all because the craftsman who had made the cabinet had covered the projecting ends of the thick canes with neat ivory knobs. But Charlie and Nora had removed one of the back ones to make a hiding place for messages and it had somehow got lost. Into the welcoming black hole the mouse had vanished, and it soon became clear that there was no way to get it out unless it chose to come. The cabinet was too large to be tipped up and shaken, moreover its little shelves were covered with fragile knick-knacks.

Charlie's suggestion that they should poke one of a pair of carved ivory chopsticks into the hole was indignantly vetoed by Nora on the grounds that it was more likely to injure the poor mouse than to dislodge it.

"But if we don't get it out before our walk, it may just come out and run away," said Charlie reasonably, "and that will mean my best penknife has just gone for nothing."

"Well, if we can't get it out, we'll have to shut it in so that it can't escape. Then when it's had time to get hungry, we'll come back and tempt it out with pieces of cheese."

This plan was agreed and Nora pushed a tiny lacquered box into the hole, wedging it in so that it would trap the mouse inside while leaving plenty of space for air to get in.

They spent the morning in Battersea Park, the wharf being empty of barges, but had to return early so that Annie could tidy her hair and change into her parlour-maid's apron and cap in time to help out at Beatrice's luncheon. To allow the garrulous Lily to wait at table would have been a recipe for disaster, and though Annie had never been trained as a parlourmaid, she was quiet and careful and rarely spilled anything.

Lily had laid the table under Beatrice's supervision and was now down in the kitchen adding to the general atmosphere of crisis which always prevailed when Cook was called upon to prepare a meal for more than four people. Beatrice was changing early in order to leave time for Annie to arrange her hair, another of her many talents.

Charlie and Nora, who were not invited, but were to have luncheon in the nursery playroom, found themselves at a loose end for half an hour, so they helped themselves to a hunk of cheese from the larder while Cook was busy bawling at Lily and decided to have a try at coaxing the mouse out.

It proved to be a fascinating game. They broke the cheese into tiny pieces and found that if they laid one outside the hole, then hid behind the heavy plush folds of the window curtains and were very quiet, the mouse would dart out and eat it. Unfortunately, this didn't help very much since at the first sign of movement, it sped back into the bamboo hole. But by trial and error, they found that with a long line of cheese crumbs (it was Cheshire and crumbled easily) they could coax it farther and farther. But always as they rushed to grab it, the mouse, which was no fool, would vanish a split second too soon. It was finally agreed that the cheese-crumb trail must be laid right across the linoleum until the unsuspecting mouse passed in front of their hiding place, where it could be intercepted and trapped in a flash under a silver dish-cover. It took quite a time to set up this complicated arrangement and then, just as they were poised behind the curtain with the silver cover at the ready, the dining-room door swung open and Beatrice swept in, radiantly nervous, leading her guests into luncheon.

The Ladies' Guild for the Support and Comfort of Our Brave Lads was composed principally of stout elderly ladies, rather than the young slim ladies whom the Brave Lads would undoubtedly have chosen to comfort them if they had had any say in the matter. Its avowed purpose was to meet and discuss ways of raising money for the noble cause. But in fact it merely provided a useful means by which ladies of good social position but limited means, like its President and Founder, Lady Crumleigh, could induce socially ambitious women like Beatrice Fanshaw to provide them with a succession of good free lunches. However, both sides were very happy with the arrangement, which from time to time even produced a few warm Balaclava helmets, knitted by the servants of the respective households; so the Guild flourished and, if it did very little good, it also did very little harm.

The ladies smiled and chatted as they took their places: Nora and Charlie made faces at each other behind the curtain and debated in whispers what they should do. As the table lay directly between the door and the window where they were hidden, there was no way of escaping without notice. They knew that to embarrass their mother during her big social event would bring a flood of reproaches and recriminations, so it seemed wisest to stay put. In any case, they had long since discovered that grown-ups on their own, when there were no children present, took on a whole new dimension of entertaining silliness, indulging in highly artificial conversations whose fatuousness bordered upon genius. Even if it had been possible to escape undetected, the chance to eavesdrop upon the Ladies' Guild luncheon was just too good to be missed.

They were rewarded with fifteen hilarious minutes on "the servant problem", during which the failings of sundry Lilys, Dorothys, Maisies and Berthas were raked over to the satisfaction of their respective employers; and another ten minutes on the relative advantages of Chelsea and Kensington as a social base, which allowed for a great deal of name-dropping and might have given the uninformed listener the impression that everyone who was anyone left visiting cards with the Ladies' Guild members. This was followed by twelve minutes on how, in the opinion of the good ladies' husbands, Lord Kitchener ought to be conducting the war (Charlie volunteered in a whisper to Nora that his best bet would be to put the Ladies' Guild in the front line and bore the enemy to death), and at last to the subject of the enemy submarine which had apparently been seen lurking in the Thames by every milkman, butcher's boy and baker's lad from Wapping to Putney. The ladies seemed agreed that, unless something was done about it, they were all in danger of being murdered in their beds at the very least, while some even made veiled hints at an even worse fate which might lie in store for them. Beatrice, anxious to flaunt her access to inside information on the subject, assured the assembled ladies that she had it on the best authority from Alfred — who was of course at the Admiralty and had actually drafted the statement to the newspapers — that there was *no* submarine in the Thames. But she was put down very promptly by Lady Crumleigh, who announced that she personally never believed anything she read in the newspapers, thus proving as Nora and Charlie had long suspected, that Cook and her Ladyship (like Judy O'Grady and the Colonel's Lady) were sisters under the skin.

By this time the meal had progressed through to its final course. This was to be the highlight of Beatrice's meal, for Lily Tompkins had been churning the handle of the ice-cream maker half the morning to produce a delectable cherry parfait. Cook grumbled and insisted that there was nothing to beat good cabinet pudding, but Beatrice knew that Lady Crumleigh had a very sweet tooth and a penchant for ice cream.

This rare delicacy, each portion crowned with a glacé cherry, arrived in the best cut-glass dishes on the best silver (plated) tray, carried by Annie with studious care. Beatrice was at last beginning to cast off the sense of foreboding that always hung about her during these functions and to reassure herself that the whole meal would pass without mishap, when disaster struck. Poor Beatrice never really knew how it happened, and indeed to understand at all it is necessary to go back for a moment to an incident as Annie was returning with the children from Battersea Park. Nora had pleaded to be allowed to gaze upon the ring once more for, since Annie was not allowed to have "followers", she could not flaunt it upon her finger but kept it on a thin cord around her neck. In pulling it out from the tight, high neck of her nursery maid's uniform, the cord had broken and she had tucked the ring away in her pocket, meaning to replace the cord when she reached home. On their return, Number 17 Tadema Terrace had been in such a state of panic and confusion, with the ice cream not setting, the cutlery needing yet another final polish, Lily sulking and Cook threatening to give notice, that she had forgotten the ring in her efforts to restore a little sanity to the scene.

Now just as she had placed Lady Crumleigh's parfait in front of her and was about to move on, balancing the tray with its fragile load upon her left hand, she felt a sudden tickling in the nose brought on by bending towards a heavily scented flower arrangement of madonna lilies which Beatrice had placed in front of her guest of honour. Uncertain whether she could suppress the irritation and anxious above all to avoid sneezing over the tray of parfaits, Annie dived into her pocket for her handkerchief. Then averting her head she quickly buried her nose in it, while unknown to her the ring, which had been caught up in the lace edging, described a neat arc and landed on top of Lady Crumleigh's parfait. There it settled itself luxuriously into the snowy coolness, the bright red stone and the glacé cherry gleaming side by side.

The sneeze when it came was modest enough to pass unnoticed amid the sparkling conversation. Annie continued on her way, placed the remaining dishes without further trouble, and withdrew to the kitchen with a sigh of relief.

Lady Crumleigh was not one of those self-denying mortals who enjoy saving the best bits until last. She scooped up both the cherries in a generous spoonful of ice cream and slipped them greedily into her mouth.

Fortunately ice cream is not a delicacy which the teeth seize upon with a powerful crunch, or she might well have cracked her false teeth and made the whole thing even worse. As it was her tongue detected the hard, metallic circle immediately, and with a cry of distaste she spat out the foreign body into the palm of her hand. Beatrice, seeing her gesture, and fearing that some marauding wasp drawn by the cherry syrup had escaped Cook's not over-vigilant eye, leaned forward wide-eyed with anxiety to see what Lady Crumleigh had found. To her astonishment she saw that it was in fact a gold ring with a brilliant red stone which lay wickedly winking and gleaming in the palm of the outraged lady's hand.

"A ring?" cried Beatrice, half overcome with mortification. "A ruby ring! But how could it possibly have fallen into the parfait? None of our servants could possibly afford such an expensive ring."

But worse was to follow. Lady Crumleigh was staring very closely at the ring. She had taken out a tiny spy-glass from her reticule and was examining the stone with the air of a pawnbroker pricing a pledge.

Then she turned upon poor Beatrice a look of haughty accusation and said, "This ring is mine! It was one of the many valuable pieces which were taken from my bedroom during the notorious robberies a year ago. I demand to know, Beatrice Fanshaw, what it is doing in your cherry parfait!"

There was a moment of horrified silence during which Beatrice thought wildly of pretending to faint in order to escape the agony of the moment. And then all the ladies began chattering at once.

Behind the curtains Charlie and Nora, who had at once recognized the ring held aloft in Lady Crumleigh's accusing hand, stared at each other in dismay. The bell was rung and Annie came unsuspectingly hurrying in to answer it.

"Annie," said Beatrice faintly, "would you please ask Cook and Lily to come up to the dining-room at once. There has been a most . . . a most . . . unfortunate occurrence."

Nora, desperate to warn Annie what was afoot, poked her head out from behind the curtain and unseen by the seated ladies, pointed furiously to the ring held aloft in Lady Crumleigh's fingers. Annie following her gesture, saw the red flash of the stone: her hand went swiftly to her pocket and found it empty. Eagerly she stepped forward and her attention now distracted from Nora, who was frantically shaking her head, said at once gratefully and apologetically, "Oh, your Ladyship, you've found my ring. Thank you so much I must have dropped it somehow while I was serving the parfait. I am so sorry, I . . . " Her voice faltered and died away as Lady Crumleigh rose suddenly to her full height, held up the ring for all to see and with her other hand outstretched in accusation cried, "Arrest that girl instantly!"

It is hard to know whom she expected to carry out this command: perhaps it was only intended to create the maximum effect, in which case it was quite successful. Annie turned white, Beatrice fainted — she had finally decided it was the only way out — and Nora and Charlie rushed from behind the curtain shouting indignantly. But such was the clamour and hubbub of excitement among the members of the Ladies' Guild, who normally led lives of stultifying boredom and were not going to miss the chance of getting hysterical once in a while, that nobody noticed them.

Chaos reigned for some time until Beatrice, finding that they were all too busy to notice that she had fainted, was forced to come round and attempt to take charge of the situation. Rising shakily to her feet, she turned to her white-faced maid and said, "Annie, I'm sure there must be some mistake. Can you really mean to lay claim to this ring?"

There was a sudden hush as the ladies waited for her answer and Annie, noticing Nora's violent head shaking (it was beginning to ache) but unable to make sense of it, said honestly, "Yes, Mum, it is mine. It was give to me by a good friend, Mum. Oh Mrs Fanshaw, I know I'm not supposed to have followers, that's why I didn't wear it, but he's ever such a nice young man and very handsome and if you met him . . . "

But Lady Crumleigh interrupted her touching testimonial. "This ring is mine," she boomed, "it was stolen from my house. It seems, Beatrice Fanshaw, that your servants are allowed to consort with thieves. Confess at once, you miserable girl, the name of this degenerate 'follower'."

"But he's not a thief! And he never would . . . he's as honest as . . . " Annie looked from Lady Crumleigh to Beatrice Fanshaw and back in obvious confusion. Then suddenly her face went blank; she stood very still for a moment and seemed to be thinking. Then she said quietly, "All right, I told a lie . . . it wasn't given to me: I found it in the street near Lady Crumleigh's house only last week. She must have dropped it there . . . "

"It's no use lying to escape your fate," said Lady Crumleigh scornfully. "The ring was stolen nearly a year ago and all the best pieces of my jewellery with it. And many other wealthy houses were robbed on the same night." She turned to Beatrice. "We are wasting time," she said. "The police must be sent for and the girl questioned until the whole gang of her accomplices has been identified. The stolen jewels must be traced and the reward, which is I believe substantial, will certainly come to me for my vigilance in unmasking the wicked girl and her . . . "

Nora could stand no more.

"She is not wicked, you pompous old woman," she shouted. "She is honest as the day is long and the ring was given to her by . . . "

"No!" the cry came from Annie, who was staring at Nora in horror. "No! Miss Nora, please, please! You know nothing about it!"

"But Annie if you tell them . . . "

"No! Please Miss Nora, you mustn't interfere. I shall do what I think is best."

Nora saw that there were tears in her eyes and realized suddenly that any fate seemed better to Annie than to confess that Jem had given her the ring, and to set the forces of the law on his trail. A terrible thought struck her: how had Jem come by the ring? Surely he could not be involved in anything dishonest. She rejected the very idea. Jem did not say a lot, but his eyes were straight and honest and she was young enough to believe implicitly in her own judgment. Either Jem had been deceived by whoever had sold him the ring or . . . perhaps Lady Crumleigh was mistaken.

"How can you be certain that is your ring?" she demanded, turning upon Annie's accuser.

"Elinor! Go to your room," said Beatrice desperately. "You are just a child: you must not . . . "

"But how does she know?" Nora turned to her mother. "There must be lots of gold rings around with a red stone. How does she know . . .?" Beatrice clutched at the straw.

"Perhaps you might be mistaken?" she suggested timorously to her enraged and indignant guest of honour.

"Mistaken! I am never mistaken and why should I have to prove my case to your daughter, Beatrice Fanshaw?"

"Well, no, of course not," said Beatrice meekly.

"However, as it happens, the ring was originally given to my Aunt Gertrude by her betrothed, who had the words 'Faithful for Ever' inscribed inside it. He was knocked down and killed by an omnibus a week later and she married another man, but that is by the by." Injecting as much drama as she could into the occasion she held the ring in her outstretched hand and raised her spy-glass to study the inscription more carefully.

And at that point, Charlie took a hand in the affair.

During the hubbub the mouse, which had so stubbornly evaded capture during Charlie and Nora's silent vigil, had suddenly emerged bold as brass and was eating its way along the trail of cheese crumbs which stretched alongside the dining-room table. Unfortunately — or fortunately as it turned out — Lady Crumleigh, while making her usual imposing entrance, had swept the line aside with the hem of her skirt so that the trail now curved sideways towards the very spot where she now stood scrutinizing the ring. Charlie had been observing the mouse's progress with bated breath lest something should disturb it before it actually reached the haven of her ladyship's skirts. Now, seeing that the moment had come when the assembled company must be distracted at all costs, he pointed downwards and shouted,

"Look! A mouse!"

Lady Crumleigh glanced down at the floor just in time to see the mouse, frightened by Charlie's cry, disappearing into the dark, sheltering haven of her petticoats. She dropped the ring and the spy-glass and, with a shriek that reached Cook and Lily in the kitchen below, she leapt on to the nearest chair beating frantically at her skirts. Her example was promptly followed by all the ladies present, except Annie, who stood as if dazed by the successsion of events, and Nora, who was trying to persuade her to make a run for it.

"No thank you, Miss Nora." Annie was quiet but firm. "I know well enough that Jem wouldn't have come by that ring dishonest, and if I should run away they will all think the worst."

At this point the dining-room door flew open and Cook and Lily burst in to add to the confusion. Cook was armed with a rolling pin and Lily with a flat-iron, and both were under the impression that the crew of the German submarine had landed and were carrying off the entire Ladies' Guild by force.

Charlie meanwhile was scrabbling on the floor after the mouse, which ran hither and thither in a frenzy. Unfortunately he trod on the spy-glass, but no one was in a fit state to notice the accident and since he finally rose to his feet clutching the cause of the confusion, he was soon the hero of the hour.

"Do take it away and put it out in the garden, dear," pleaded Beatrice, who was not yet sufficiently recovered to ask herself how it had found its way into the dining-room in the first place.

"Yes, of course, mother," said Charlie angelically and added, "you may come down now ladies: there is nothing to fear!"

Then he made his escape while the going was good.

It took some time to convince all the ladies and to coax them down off their chairs and even longer to persuade Cook that the Huns were not responsible for the pandemonium.

At last, when all was comparatively quiet and Lady Crumleigh was ready to resume her identification of the ring, it proved impossible to find it. The floor was searched and the table crockery: the parfaits, now sadly melted, were dredged without results. Lady Crumleigh demanded that Annie should be searched and she willingly submitted, but the ring was nowhere to be found.

"It was hilarious!" Nora told Charlie in the quiet of the nursery five minutes later. "Lady Crumleigh wanted to call the police, but mother wriggled out of it by saying that they couldn't be certain that it was the same ring that had been stolen. She said she must wait and tell father when he returns this evening and leave him to decide what to do. There was a terrible scene with everyone talking at once and at last it was agreed that Annie should be locked in her room until father comes home. All the ladies swept out, Lady Crum says she will never darken our doorstep again, and mother is in her room with a fit of the vapours."

"Marvellous!" said Charlie, heartlessly. "Pity I missed the fun."

There was a long pause while they both savoured the memories.

Then at last Nora said, "You've got the ring, of course?"

"Of course," agreed Charlie. "I thought I had better nobble it before Lady Crum could prove whether or not it was really hers."

"And was it?" asked Nora.

"Look," said Charlie simply and handed it to her.

In tiny letters around the inside curve, Nora could just make out the words: "Faithful for Ever".

As soon as the coast was clear, Nora and Charlie hurried up to Annie's room and had an urgent whispered conference through the key-hole, the outcome of which was a unanimous decision that Jem Kitson must be told and the sooner the better.

"Don't worry, Annie!" said Charlie. "You can safely leave everything in our hands."

"Thank you very much, I'm sure, Master Charlie," said Annie. It did seem to Charlie that her voice sounded rather less confident than he would have expected, but through the key-hole it was hard to be sure. Nora looked in on Beatrice, who was lying in her darkened bedroom with a cold compress over her eyes and a bottle of smelling salts clasped in her limp hand.

"Are you feeling better?" asked Nora in her most sympathetic voice. Charlie gallantly resisted the temptation to shout suddenly in his mother's ear and see her galvanized into hysterical action.

"My head is very painful," said Beatrice weakly. "I think I shall try to sleep a little."

"Oh yes, what a good idea," said Nora sweetly, "and shall I ask Annie . . . I mean Lily, to wake you in a couple of hours' time with a tray of tea."

"What a kind thought . . . " Beatrice struggled to assume some responsibility for her children, "And you and Charlie?"

"Oh, I thought we might go out for a walk with Nanny Parker," said Nora, "so that Charlie shall not disturb you with his noise."

Beatrice nodded her approval and fell into a light dreaming doze in which she seemed doomed to face a succession of trying social occasions while inappropriately clothed, and with Charlie and Nora popping up in the most unexpected places, somewhat larger than life size, to laugh at her discomforture.

Nora put on her hat and Charlie his cap and jacket and they collected Nanny Parker from her room.

Cook was safely occupied in the kitchen with her feet up and a glass of medicinal brandy. But Lily Tompkins was outside leaning on the area railings, having intercepted the milkman's lad on his afternoon round to regale him with the scandal of the day's events.

She glanced officiously at Charlie and Nora as they bounced Nanny Parker down the front steps. They were both holding the back of the bath chair and were having difficulty synchronizing the descent of each step so that the old lady tossed from side to side like a leaf in a storm.

"You watch what you're doing with Nanny Parker there," said Lily making no effort to help them.

"Yes, you be careful," added the milkman's lad equally unmoved. "You don't want the old girl tipped out into the gutter."

But Nanny Parker roused herself unexpectedly and shouted "You stop flirting and get back to your work, young Lily Tompkins!" which rendered Lily speechless with indignation and enabled Charlie and Nora to make a hasty escape along Tadema Terrace.

"Interfering old . . . " began Lily when she had regained the power of speech, but she thought better of it and contented herself with poking out her tongue. By the time it occurred to her to wonder if Charlie and Nora were supposed to be taking Nanny Parker out by themselves in the middle of the afternoon, they were rounding the corner into Lots Road. She shrugged her shoulders and resumed her highly coloured version of the fateful luncheon party.

Charlie and Nora hurried on down to the wharf, hoping against hope that they would find the *Windhawk* there.

Eleven

The *Blackbird* had unloaded her small freight of bricks in a couple of hours and Batty Fred, who found that the cheese and chutney sandwiches had given him a terrible thirst, suddenly remembered an old friend living near by whom he hadn't seen for years and hurried off ashore to visit him.

"I bet his old friend keeps the nearest pub," said Daniel. "He'll probably come back the worse for wear."

"Oh, do you think so?" said Rosie. "Perhaps I shouldn't have let him go. Still," she added, "it does mean we've got the boat to ourselves. Now we can play pirates."

Ten minutes later, Daniel was tied to the mast and feeling rather foolish when he suddenly became aware of the fact that he was being watched. Up at the top of the wharf steps stood a tall girl with reddish hair, and a boy a little younger holding the handle of a bath chair in which sat a very old lady. They were staring down at the *Blackbird* with an expression which he could only describe as one of resentment as if they considered that she had no right to be where she was.

Daniel felt at a distinct disadvantage with his hands tied. "Rosie," he hissed, "untie my hands, there's a good girl."

"I've only just tied them up," said Rosie reasonably, "and anyway I'm not very good at untying."

"Please, Rosie."

"Why?"

"Well, I may be wrong but I think we've got visitors." The boy and the red-headed girl were having a whispered conference and their unwavering stares left no doubt as to the subject of it.

"Who?" said Rosie, "Where?" and then as a sudden thought struck her, "Oh, Danny, it's not them from the orphanage, is it? They haven't come to get me?"

Daniel considered. The old lady looked too old to be running an orphanage, and the two children were too well dressed to be inmates.

"I don't think so," he said, "but you'd better untie me just in case."

Rosie suddenly became very good at untying knots and when he was free Daniel hurried about the deck tidying ropes and doing his best to make it clear that he was really the barge's mate and not just a boy playing pirates on board with his little sister. It wasn't very successful, because after watching him for several minutes the tall girl suddenly called:

"Hey, boy! Is there anyone on board."

Daniel glared at her. "Course there is," he said, "there's me, and my sister . . . and Joxer," he added as the dog, hearing a strange voice, hurried up from below and began to bark noisily.

The girl could barely conceal her scorn. "No, silly, I mean someone who's in charge," she explained. "Where is the Skipper?"

"He's gone ashore." Daniel's answer was curt: he was smarting under the insult of being called silly by a bean-pole of a girl with a snooty accent.

"Where's the mate then?"

"I'm the mate," said Daniel, his mouth setting into a cross line.

"Oh, do stop playing games. We need to see someone who's in charge. It's important and we're in a hurry."

At this point Rosie decided that, orphanage or no orphanage, she could not allow this disrespect for her brother's rank to continue any longer.

"I don't know who you are," she told Nora indignantly, "but you've got very bad manners. This is my brother Daniel and he is the mate of the *Blackbird*, so you can talk to him if you want to as long as you're a bit more polite. Otherwise you'll have to wait and talk to Batty Fred when he gets back, only it won't do you much good, 'cos his friend's probably got a pub and he'll come back worn out."

"Oh!" said Nora, left temporarily speechless by this sudden outburst, and before she could sort it out enough to answer, Charlie said admiringly:

"Are you really the barge's mate?"

"Yes," Daniel was mollified by the hint of respect in his voice, "Yes, I am," he repeated rather more firmly and he added, "you can come aboard if you like."

Charlie didn't need to be told twice. He was down the steps and on to the *Blackbird*'s deck in a moment, leaving Nora out on a limb.

"How long have you been a mate? And how did you get the job? And how old are you?" he asked, feeling towards Daniel the same sort of wistful envy that Daniel himself felt in the presence of Jem Kitson.

"He's twelve," said Rosie proudly just as Daniel was opening his mouth to say that he was fourteen.

"Twelve! Gosh, I thought you'd have to be much older. Why I shall be ten next month, that means I've only got two years to wait! Did you hear that Nora? In another two years I can . . . "

"Never mind that," said Nora, cross at being left out of the conversation. "What about Annie? You seem to have forgotten that we are looking for Jem."

"Jem?" Daniel turned his head at the familiar name.

"Yes, Jem Kitson. He's a friend of ours and we have to get in touch with him urgently." Nora's voice was cool; she was still smarting under Rosie's criticism of her manners, especially as she did feel she had been rather rude.

But to claim friendship with Jem was a key which opened all doors with Daniel. He turned upon Nora a smile that was like sunshine.

"But Jem is a friend of ours too!" he said delightedly. "In fact he was the one that helped me to get this job." He had long since forgotten what a dirty trick it had seemed at the time.

"We were hoping to find him here," explained Charlie. "We have to find him as soon as we can."

"Well he won't be here until tomorrow, or late tonight at the very earliest," Daniel told them. "The *Windhawk* is up at Putney waiting for rigging repairs. Why do you want to see him?"

"Well . . . " Nora racked her brains to know what to do. They could hardly leave Nanny Parker on the wharfside and go off to Putney. She wasn't even sure how to get there and then mother would have a fit if they were gone too long.

Rosie took a hand. She had abandoned the idea of being a pirate, at least for the moment, and had decided to play tea-parties since they had the *Blackbird* all to themselves and visitors had appeared so opportunely.

"If you'd like to come downstairs," she told Nora and Charlie rather grandly, "I'll make you a cup of tea and you can tell us all about your trouble."

"Below," said Daniel.

Rosie frowned at him. "Below what?"

"Go below. You don't go downstairs on boats, you go below."

Rosie tossed her head impatiently and ignored him. "Would you like a cup of tea?" she asked Nora winningly.

And Nora and Charlie, who never missed a chance to inspect one of the barges, said that they would.

It was all very well for Rosie, thought Daniel, watching her as she supervised the introductions, waved Nora and Charlie graciously towards a seat on the old bunks, and filled the kettle with a scoop from the fresh-water bucket. She seemed to think that life was a succession of games to play, with herself to organize them and everyone else to join in and play whatever she had chosen. Even Batty Fred, without his knowledge, had figured so far as the hunter in hide and seek, a patient in doctors and nurses and a sort of friendly uncle in mothers and fathers. As a result she had a completely false picture of his character, and if as Daniel suspected, he was now filling himself up with alcohol at the nearest public house, he would return in no mood to join in the game of entertaining visitors, which Rosie had now embarked upon. He therefore felt very uneasy with the two strangers on board, for to have invited them below while the *Blackbird*'s Skipper was away seemed to him a course set straight for disaster. But he consoled himself with the thought that Batty Fred would almost certainly stay glued to the bar until closing time and by then the two visitors would be long since gone. To hurry things up he asked, "What do you want Jem Kitson for?"

Charlie and Nora began to explain about Annie and the ring. It was a tale which could have been told quite quickly but since they were staying for tea, and since the events of the afternoon were fresh in their memories and this was the first chance they had had to recount them and relive the blissful memories of the rout of the Ladies' Guild, the two Fanshaws did the story proud. Even the mouse was produced from Charlie's pocket at the appropriate moment in the tale, whereupon Rosie gave up playing hostess to sit and nurse it on her lap and Daniel found himself deputizing as mug-washer and tea-maker.

"Oh you poor little mouse, you must have been so scared," said Rosie, stroking its quivering white nose sympathetically, as Charlie recounted the panic and screams of Lady Crumleigh and her band.

"Not nearly as scared as they were!" Charlie assured her. "But anyway the main thing was that old Lady Crum dropped the ring and I managed to nobble it before anyone could prove one way or the other whether it was the stolen one and so now . . . "

"And now," interrupted Nora, who felt that he was

getting more that his fair share of attention, "we have to find Jem Kitson and try to discover where it came from, before father gets home and calls the police and Annie ends up in prison."

Daniel stirred the tea in the old chipped tea-pot and poured it out. In spite of the breakage money, which he had deducted from Daniel's wages, Batty Fred had never replaced any of the smashed crockery and they were now down to two chipped mugs, a cracked cup and a small stained pudding basin.

"Have you got the ring with you?" he asked cautiously, when he had distributed these unappetizing containers. Although Charlie had not bothered to describe the ring, Daniel had been seized with a growing feeling as he listened to the story that the ring which was at the cause of all the trouble had a wicked red gleam at the heart of it.

"Yes, of course," said Charlie, "I couldn't leave it at home in case the police came and searched the place." He fished it out of his pocket and held it out to Daniel, but it was promptly intercepted by Rosie. She returned the mouse, in which she had suddenly lost interest, and popped the ring on to her finger, waving it about admiringly and watching with fascination as it flashed and sparkled.

Daniel stared at it in silence for a moment and then said, "You don't need to find Jem, I can tell you where he got it from."

The other three stared at him.

"Where?" asked Nora and Charlie in unison.

"He got it from me."

This revelation caused something of a stir, as indeed he had hoped it would.

"From you?" asked Nora, and Charlie added, "Well, where did you get it from?"

Daniel hesitated. He was so proud of his new brave image as barge mate, so flattered by Charlie's obvious envy and admiration, that it came hard to have to admit that only a couple of weeks before he had been part of a gang of boys who sorted through old garbage for half a crown a week. But he could see no way of avoiding the confession; the alternative of having them think that he had stolen the ring was even worse.

So he told them the whole story, generously glossing over the rather underhand trick by which Jem had induced him to part with the ring, since it seemed to have turned out for the best.

"You mean you sold the stolen ring to Jem?" asked Nora.

"Yes," said Daniel.

"That's fencing," said Charlie. "Dealing in stolen property is fencing. You could go to prison for years and years for that."

This was a thought which had never occurred to Daniel.

"But I didn't know it was stolen," he protested. "I didn't even know it was valuable. I just found it in the rough stuff. The lads always keep any bits that they find . . . "

"Well, of course, we believe you but will the police?"

"The police!" Daniel was quite naturally becoming anxious at the way things were going.

"Well, yes," said Nora. "Father is bound to call the police and when we explain how Annie came to have the ring . . . "

"Then don't tell them!"

"But we shall have to," Nora raised her voice indignantly. "Unless we can prove that she came by it honestly, Annie Batey may end up in prison!"

And it was, of course, precisely at that moment that the cabin went dark as the light from the scuttle hatch was obscured and the squat shape of Batty Fred loomed into view.

He had, indeed, as Daniel had guessed made straight for the nearest pub, a decrepit gin house called the Sailor's Return. But after a couple of pints, his conscience, which had previously lain dormant for at least twenty years, began to prickle uneasily like a limb regaining its feeling after a long period of cramp. Rosie's presence on board gave him an unfamiliar sense of responsibility. The picture of himself lurching drunkenly back on board in the early hours seemed somehow reprehensible when he imagined it seen through her eyes. Would she be distressed? He tried to picture her weeping, but it didn't seem to fit. More likely, he decided, she would be very cross with him and a mental picture of an enraged and scornful Rosie was not one he cared to dwell upon. So he had drained the last of his mug and decided to go back on board before he was too far gone to refuse another. He arrived back to hear excited voices coming from the after-cabin, and putting his head in the scuttle to investigate was just in time to hear Nora mention the awful fate that awaited his beloved niece Annie.

"Prison!" he roared. "My Annie in prison! And why would that be may I ask? And what would you know about it, young woman? And what would you two be doing trespassing on my barge anyway?"

Daniel turned pale; Charlie and Nora looked uncomfortable; Rosie took charge.

"They are not trespassing, Mr Batey, because I invited them to tea," she said firmly. "Would you like a cup? And how is your poor hand?"

"Never you mind that . . . I mean, well yes I would. That is to say . . . thank you kindly, it's much better I'm sure," Batty Fred paused uncertainly and, like a charging rhinoceros stopped in its tracks and lacking the time and space to get up speed again, he found that Rosie's interruption had somehow taken the momentum out of his fierce indignation.

"What's all this about my Annie, then?" he asked anxiously.

"Nora and Charlie will explain all that," said Rosie, "if you will just stop shouting at people and give them a chance. Now do sit down and listen."

Batty Fred sat down like a deflated balloon and Nora explained that Annie was in trouble for having the ring which Daniel had found in the rough stuff.

"Well, what you want to give it to my Annie for?" Fred turned on Daniel indignantly. "She's a good, well-brought-up girl, my poor dead brother's child, and honest as the day is long."

"But I didn't know it was stolen," protested Daniel, "and anyway I didn't give it to her, I sold it to . . . " He paused at the last moment realizing the effect that the hated name would have on Batty Fred's already uncertain temper.

But Nora, missing the connection between the bewildered old Skipper and Annie's tale of the warring Fred and Punchy, finished the sentence for him.

"He sold it to Jem Kitson. It was Jem who gave it to Annie."

The colour drained suddenly from Batty Fred's face until even his nose was reduced to a shade of pale pink more suited to a young girl's cheek. He opened his mouth once or twice but no sound came out. The children watched with interest. Then the colour came flooding back again and grew in intensity until even his neck seemed suffused with a carmine glow. His mouth continued to open and shut soundlessly and it seemed that unless words were forthcoming before too long, he was in danger of disintegrating under the force of his own frustration.

"Are you all right?" asked Nora, her voice betraying more curiosity than concern.

With a last supreme effort, Batty Fred forced out the words, "Jem . . . Kitson?" he squeaked, strangling the name as he would undoubtedly have liked to strangle its owner. "Jem Kitson gave a ring . . . to my Annie?" In spite of his generally low opinion of his fellow man, he seemed quite unable to credit that even Punchy Kitson's son could possibly sink so low.

"Yes," said Nora brightly. "It was terribly romantic! They were sitting side by side on the *Windhawk*, I saw it all, and . . . "

"My niece Annie . . . was on the *Windhawk*?" He made it sound as if the bird for which the barge had been named was some appalling species of vulture with unmentionable habits.

"Yes," said Nora again, not realizing that each repetition of that simple word was like a dagger thrust deep into Batty Fred's heart and turned painfully. "Yes, she was moored up right here, and they were sitting on the hatch-cover side by side and . . . "

"Oh, Annie! Annie!" The cry came from Batty Fred with such anguish that his unreasonable hatred seemed to take on a sort of nobility, like Lear in his madness. "After your Ma brought you up so decent . . . and when I sent you to live in Chelsea among respectable people away from them scum of the river . . . why my poor dead brother must be turning in his grave!"

"But Annie said her father was a barge Skipper himself," said Charlie reasonably, "and her grandfather before him."

"And Chelsea people are not particularly respectable," said Nora perceptively. "They may be richer, but they're no better than the river people."

"Some," said Charlie, thinking of the unscrupulous Lady Crumleigh, "are a lot worse!"

"Ah," Batty Fred seized upon this revelation. "That's what it is then . . . she's been corrupted! My Annie had been corrupted by them awful Chelsea people. They told me she wouldn't 'ave no followers . . . " His voice began to rise again.

"But she has not been corrupted," shouted Nora beginning to lose patience with him. "She's as sweet and as good as she always was. And Jem Kitson is a very nice young man, and they love each other. I don't know what you're making so much fuss about."

"Love? That's not love! That Jem Kitson is just like his father . . . he's been leading my Annie astray just to get back at me . . . "

"Oh don't be so stupid, you silly old man. What would you know about love? You're old and mean and I bet you can't even remember what love is like — that's if you were ever in love."

"Me, not know about love!" Batty Fred was most indignant. "Why, I've been a martyr to it all my life. It's been for love that I've lived alone and neglected all these years since that devil Punchy Kitson stole my Dora from me!"

"Well if he was anything like Jem when he was young, I'm not surprised she married him instead of you," said Nora, riding rough-shod over all Batty Fred's illusions. "Any girl in her right mind would. After all, every woman has a right to choose her own husband. You're not a martyr at all, you're just a bad loser!"

Daniel who had been listening to Nora holding her own against Batty Fred with awe and admiration, decided reluctantly that it had gone far enough.

"In any case," he put in soothingly, "that isn't really the problem. We have to find a way to clear Annie's name so that she won't be sent to prison."

"Well that's easy enough," said Batty Fred spitefully. "I shall tell the police that it was Jem Kitson what give 'er the ring and let them put him in prison."

"But I found the ring," said Daniel, "it wasn't Jem's fault."

"Serves him right for giving it to my Annie!" Batty Fred seemed to relish the idea of putting Jem Kitson where he would be out of Annie's reach.

"What about Daniel? He might go to prison too," Charlie pointed out, hoping that Batty Fred might have more sympathy for his own crewman.

But the old man was feeling thoroughly mean. "Only got 'imself to blame if he does!" he said unreasonably.

Rosie was furious. Raising one small tightly clenched fist she punched Batty Fred severely in the knee, shouting, "Don't you dare get my brother Daniel put in prison, you horrid old man!" and then, her anger stemming mostly from a terrible fear of losing the only member of her family left to her, she added, "And I thought you were my friend!" and burst into a flood of tears.

Everyone was horrified. Daniel knelt to comfort her saying, "Now then, Rosie, you know Mr Batey wouldn't really let them put me in prison . . . it's only his way of talking. Of course he's your friend, and we're all going to find a way of saving Annie without any of us going to prison, aren't we Mr Batey?"

Batty Fred, overwhelmed with guilt at the sight of Rosie's anger and distress, swallowed hard. "Yerse . . . of course," he said. "Now don't you take on so, Rosie," and rubbed ruefully at his aching knee.

"But how are we going to do it?" asked Charlie.

There was a long thoughtful silence, broken only by the fading snuffles of Rosie's tears. And then Daniel said quietly, "I think the only way we can do it is to catch the jewel thieves, the ones who stole the ring from Lady whatsername."

They all stared at him.

"If what she says is true," he went on, "I mean that she didn't just lose the ring but had it stolen along with a lot of other stuff, then I think the loot was hidden in the rough stuff and it may still be there."

"In all that rubbish? Why would they do that?" Charlie was not impressed by Daniel's theory.

"To get it away from London, of course," and as

Charlie shrugged disparagingly, Daniel went on, "Way back last year the police searched a whole bargeload of rough stuff at Otterham but they didn't find anything. Now they must have had a reason for thinking something was there: maybe someone tipped them off. But supposing there was some kind of a mix up and they searched the wrong barge. Suppose even the thieves have lost track of the jewels and they're still in there."

"It sounds a bit far-fetched," said Charlie, "and even if the jewels were there that doesn't help us to catch the thieves."

"Let me finish," said Daniel. "I think the thieves know that they're somewhere in the piles and they're hunting for them. Rosie and I saw a strange man searching through the rough-stuff piles last Sunday afternoon, didn't we Rosie?"

"Yes," said Rosie. "His hands tasted really nasty!"

"He was there for hours," Daniel went on, "in the drizzling rain poking around the heaps until he finally gave up and sloped off to the pub. I don't think he found anything, but he could have been one of the gang."

And then to his surprise, Batty Fred spoke up. "Last Sunday evening . . . " he said thoughtfully, "I seen 'im . . . in the Anchor and Hope, flash London bully he was, boasting about his underworld friends and making eyes at my Dora." The crime of stealing Dora's attention was a much greater offence in Batty Fred's eyes than any mere jewel theft. "I'd like to lay my hands on him one of these dark nights."

"That's just what we must do," said Daniel eagerly, "if we want to clear Annie without getting Jem into trouble — or me either, come to that."

"Couldn't you just search through the heaps and find the loot?" suggested Nora.

Daniel groaned. "It would take for ever," he said, "there are eight boys sifting through it all day long and they just keep piling up more. Of course the boys will find the rest of it one day, if it's there, but it will be too late for Annie. If we lie in wait tonight and that fellow comes back, we could take him by surprise. Then we might be able to prove to the police that the jewels were hidden there and that Jem and Annie and I had nothing to do with the robbery."

"Oh Nora, can we go too?" Charlie was thrilled at the prospect of tangling with a gang of dangerous criminals.

"Oh don't be silly, Charlie," said Nora crossly — she was cross because she badly wanted to go to but she was old enough to know that life is never that simple. "We can't just sail away leaving Nanny Parker stranded on the wharf."

"We could take her with us," suggested Charlie, not very hopefully.

"And what would happen when we didn't get back from our walk? Mother would call the police; they would be dragging the river, it would be the most awful scene. As for father, it might be the last straw and you know what he would do."

"Send us away to school," said Charlie gloomily. This fearsome threat which would separate them from each other and from their beloved river, was the ultimate sanction with which Alfred Fanshaw prevented his children from getting hopelessly out of line.

Daniel turned to Batty Fred. "We must go down river at once, Mr Batey," he said urgently.

"Can't," said Batty Fred. "Tide don't turn for a couple of

hours. And in any case, *Blackbird* couldn't make the Medway on one tide."

"We did it coming up."

"We 'ad a good fair wind behind us, it's dropped away now. And we towed up from Woolwich."

"We can tow down again," said Daniel. "By the time the tide turns in a couple of hours, we could be way down river. And as for the wind, well when it drops away suddenly after a blow like that, it'll come again like as not from the other quarter."

Charlie gazed at him in admiration of this display of weatherlore and even Batty Fred seemed reluctantly impressed. "What do you know about wind and tide," he said disparagingly.

"Quite a lot," said Daniel eagerly. "I learnt it from . . . er . . . from my Dad," he ended feebly. He had been about to say Jem and Punchy but realized in the nick of time that information from such a source would be instantly dismissed as useless.

Batty Fred seemed unconvinced, so Daniel resorted to blatant flattery.

"There aren't many Skippers who could make the Medway by tonight in an old stumpy," he said turning to the others, "but I reckon Mr Batey could do it."

But Batty Fred saw through the flattery and just scowled.

Nora narrowed her eyes cunningly and tried a different tack. "Nonsense," she said contemptuously. "He couldn't possibly make it. But the *Windhawk* will be down this evening and I'll bet Jem and Punchy can do it."

"Yes," agreed Charlie. "When we tell them what's happened, she'll pass this old tub before she makes the

Lower Hope." He wasn't at all sure where the Lower Hope was, but he had picked up the name from Punchy and liked the sound of it.

Batty Fred reacted like a bad-tempered bull which has been poked with a stick.

"You two brats get off my boat this minute!" he yelled to Charlie and Nora. "I'll show you who's the better sailorman. You, boy!" to Daniel, "Make her ready while I go for a tug. Who says the *Blackbird* can't make the Medway on one ebb? Why them Kitsons won't get so much as a whiff of the wind up our backsides!" And in a moment he was away along the wharf.

Daniel grinned at Charlie and Nora. "Thanks," he said.

"It was a pleasure," said Nora truthfully.

Half-an-hour later Nora and Charlie stood with Nanny Parker on Battersea Bridge and watched the *Blackbird* with Batty Fred at the helm steering her way downstream behind the tug, until she vanished out of sight among the busy traffic of the river.

"I still wish we could have gone with her," said Charlie mournfully. "We shall miss all the fun."

Nora turned her head slowly and Charlie saw that she was wearing her enigmatic smile. It gave her the look of a cat which had been at the cream jug, and always meant that she was up to something.

"Go downstream in that pathetic old wreck?" she said derisively. Don't be stupid, Charlie. We're going down on the *Windhawk*."

Twelve

The spring tide which on the previous day had carried the
Blackbird up the Thames towards Chelsea swept her
downstream again to the mouth of the Medway, where it
slackened and turned with her as she made her way up her
home river. Now she was forced to tack laboriously
against the wind, which had previously favoured her on
her journey downstream. They had held their tow as far as
Gravesend, but from there on it had been a hard but
exhilarating sail. Daniel had been forced to admit to
himself that years of sailing backwards and forwards over
the few miles between the brick yard and the mud hole,
had done nothing to lessen Batty Fred's skill as a
sailorman, indeed he had risen to the challenge like a man
reborn. Unfortunately the poor old *Blackbird* could not so
easily throw off the years of neglect: her spars creaked
ominously and her patched canvas threatened to rip apart
under the strain. There had been more than one moment
on the way when Daniel had feared for their safety and had

ventured to suggest to his Skipper that they might ease off a little. But Rosie, who did not know enough about barges to sense the danger, had sided with Batty Fred and over-ruled his caution. It was therefore with a considerable sense of relief that Daniel at last made the *Blackbird* secure to a buoy in the creek by the Lower Field. The tide was too low to bring her into the mud wharf, instead it was necessary to moor off and row ashore.

Already the sun was setting behind the brickyard buildings turning the high cowls of bricks to black silhouettes. It painted the rough-stuff piles with a rosy light that glowed in the distance and put Daniel in mind of the heather-clad mountains in an old print of Highland cattle that hung in the parlour at home. The thought of that small cosy room and his mother bending to light the evening lamp came to him like a sharp pain, made even keener by the guilt of realizing that in the confusion of the preceding hours he had hardly given her a thought. What if she were lying in her strange hospital bed calling for him in her delirium . . . he forced himself to put the thought to the back of his mind. Tomorrow he would go in search of news, but for the present he had more than enough to worry about. I must be mad, he thought, to be going into this with Batty Fred and Rosie — it was impossible to predict at any moment what either of them would do. Now if it had only been Jem and Punchy . . . with those two beside him he would have tackled anything.

It had been decided on the journey down that they should lie in wait in sight of the rough-stuff piles and if the dark man came again . . . precisely what they would do then had not been specified, since to be truthful none of them was at all sure, though Rosie saw him trussed up and

153

subjected to her skilful cross-questioning, which she had no doubt would soon worm the truth out of him. But at least the first part of the plan had been agreed and Batty Fred was preparing for the long vigil with the single-minded obsessiveness of childhood. This was not so surprising as it might seem, for he was in many ways that not uncommon phenomenon an elderly child. It was as if the great shock of Dora's marriage to Punchy all those years before had not so much curdled his wits – as was popularly believed around the Lower Field – but had in some way forced him back into an eternal childhood. He had refused to accept a maturity in which it might be necessary to see Dora's choice as a reflection upon his own worth. Instead he had chosen a perpetual state of childishness in which he could accuse and hate and sulk quite openly, and in which Dora, now for ever beyond his reach as sweetheart and wife, could assume the role of comforting mother to his grieving child.

So it was that, in pursuit of the jewel thieves who had however unwittingly put his Annie in jeopardy, he set to work like some overgrown boy: with much boasting and swaggering and fearsome threats as to what he would do with the varmints when he laid his hands on them. Any other grown man would probably have approached the police directly with his story and left the matter in their hands; or he would have recruited some other strong men to lie in wait with him. He would certainly not have considered Daniel and Rosie as suitable companions for what might turn out to be a dangerous adventure. But Batty Fred treated Daniel much as if they were two lads involved in a wild escapade.

It is true that he did tell Rosie rather condescendingly

that she must stay behind on the *Blackbird*, but this was not so much because she was too young to be endangered, but for the reason any average boy might have given: because she was a girl. Rosie treated this instruction as she would have handled any suggestion which she considered too stupid to be worth answering: she quite simply ignored it. And when Daniel and Batty Fred were in position, crouched inside the half-shell of an old ship's lifeboat which lay hulked on the saltings beyond the rough-stuff piles, Rosie was right beside them.

Batty Fred was armed with a belaying pin. His first choice had been a marlin spike, but Daniel had felt that to be within range of the old man when he was armed with such a lethal weapon was a risk he was not prepared to take, and he had managed to talk him out of it. Daniel had a length of rope which was to be used to tie up the offender once Batty Fred had temporarily stunned him. Rosie, on the other hand, armed herself with a packet of her doorstep sandwiches, which as the long evening wore on proved to be by far the most sensible choice, since there was no sign of any movement from the rough-stuff piles and hunger and thirst soon became the greatest enemies.

Batty Fred grew bored after the first half-hour and suggested that it might be best if he just nipped down to the Anchor and Hope and see if there was any sign of the stranger in the bar. But Rosie said, "No, I don't think so," very firmly and the child in Batty Fred seemed to accept her authority. He sulked for a while and he had to be restored to good humour with a couple of sandwiches.

From time to time they would hear footsteps in the distance coming from the direction of the Lower Field and then they would become tense for action, waiting with bated breath to see if the sound would stop as it reached the rough stuff. But always the footsteps continued on unchecked, and peering cautiously out in the fading light they would see the figure of one of the Lower Field's brickies, making his way down to Dora's for an evening pint or two.

Time passed and the strain of the day's excitement, the exhaustion of the long sail, began to tell upon them. As the light faded, Daniel found it harder and harder to tell whether his eyes were open or shut. He thought wistfully of the *Windhawk* and Jem and Punchy . . . if only they had arrived in time. His mind drifted away . . . soon there was no sound but a repetitive whistling which could have been the wind through the cracks in the timber. The moon, briefly silvering the darkness a moment later, revealed the touching picture of Batty Fred peacefully snoring, with Rosie leaning comfortably against his shoulder and Daniel leaning comfortably against her, all equally dead to the world.

In fact, Jem and Punchy were closer than Daniel thought, though to say where would be to get ahead of my story. We must first go back to the moment when Nora revealed to Charlie on the bridge at Battersea her determination to go down river with the *Windhawk*.

"Suppose she doesn't stop at Chelsea," Charlie had objected as they sped the protesting Nanny Parker bumpily back along Cheyne Walk.

"We must signal from the nursery window."

"They'll think we're just waving."

"We'll do SOS and get Annie to wave with us," Nora told him. "Then when they come alongside, we'll rush down and tell them what's happened. After all it's no use leaving the hunt for the jewel thieves to that stupid old man."

She darted suddenly across the road, making a team of dray horses swerve. The driver of a high-seated yellow automobile pulled on his brake, nearly throwing the elegantly veiled lady beside him into the gutter, but Nora didn't even notice.

"But they won't let us go with them, anyway," said Charlie gloomily as they jerked the bath chair up the kerb on the far side. "And why are we hurrying," he asked, as they raced along Cremorne Road and turned into Tadema Terrace, "she won't come down river before four o'clock when the tide turns."

Little knowall, thought Nora crossly, but she just tossed her red hair and said haughtily, "And we shall need every minute of the time to lay our plans."

It was an exaggeration. They tucked Nanny Parker safely away in the old nursery with a decanter of port from the dining-room to keep her quiet. Then they checked upon the other ladies in the house. Beatrice was still prostrated on her bed with the blinds down; Cook was similarly sulking in her room with "one of her heads" because no one had thought to thank her for all the work she had put into the disastrous luncheon party. Only Lily Tompkins was enjoying herself. After coping with the mountain of dishes, she had gone for her afternoon off, which she was passing very agreeably with the milkman's boy at the band concert in Battersea Park.

It was no problem to obtain the key to Annie's room during a sympathy call on the unsuspecting Beatrice, but persuading Annie to escape was more of a problem.

"Why should I run away if I am innocent?" she

protested reasonably. "It will only make them think the worst, Miss Nora. I must stay and explain things to your father when he gets in."

"And what about Jem? He'll go to jail for handling stolen property even if you don't," Charlie told her heartlessly.

"It couldn't have been stolen, Master Charlie, Jem would never . . . "

"Oh, but it was, it's got the inscription inside just like old Lady Crum said it had," and Charlie dived into his pocket to fetch it out and prove his point.

But the ring was no longer there. He checked his other pockets — waking up the mouse which was dozing peacefully — but with no better luck. He tried to remember when he had had it last.

"Show her then," said Nora impatiently.

"I seem to have lost it," admitted Charlie sheepishly.

"Oh, really Charlie! Isn't that just typical!" Nora cast up her eyes despairingly. "Well, anyway, Annie dear, he's right. I saw it myself: 'Faithful for Ever'. And we know how Jem got it: he bought it from a boy called Daniel who crews for your Uncle Fred, and he found it in a pile of rubbish."

"Daniel that is, not your uncle, and it wasn't rubbish it was rough stuff," put in Charlie feeling that he was making matters clearer.

Poor Annie only looked more bewildered than ever. However, ten minutes later she had somehow managed to sort out the facts in spite of Nora and Charlie's efforts to explain them, and learning that her Uncle Fred had departed to tackle the jewel thieves, if they were to be found, aided only by Daniel and Rosie, she was forced to agree that it would be safer to alert Jem and Punchy to the impending disaster and send them in pursuit.

"But then we must come straight back here and wait to tell your father everything when he gets in," Annie told them. "I won't have it said that I ran away because I was guilty."

"No, of course not, Annie," said Nora soothingly. "But just in case father should return while we are down at the wharf, I'm writing him a letter to explain. I mean we don't want him to come charging down to the wharf with half a dozen policemen, do we," and she grinned conspiratorially at Charlie, for she had no intention of returning and the letter was meant to tone down the clamour of the hue and cry when their father found they had gone.

The *Windhawk* came down from Putney the moment the tide slackened and turned. With her spars laid low along her deck to shoot the bridges, Punchy and Jem rigged the small bridge sail and steered her down on the ebb.

Glancing up as always to the back of Number 17 Tadema Terrace in the hope of catching a glimpse of Annie as he went past, Jem was surprised to see her waving a large white sheet from the nursery window. Nora's voice could be heard shouting faintly across the distance and Charlie seemed to be flashing a small round mirror into the sun.

Jem turned to Punchy. "Here Dad, what do you make of that?"

"Reckon they wants us to go into the wharf," said Punchy impassively.

"Tricky with no way on," said Jem.

They waved back good-humouredly.

159

The trio at the window redoubled their efforts and Punchy began to detect a pattern in the patches of light.

"You reckon that's meant to be a message?" he asked Jem.

"Dunno. They do look a bit steamed up all of 'em."

"Better go in," said Punchy. "Maybe pick up a freight of rough stuff and still be away on the ebb. Fresh breeze westerly: we'll make the Medway on the flood with no bother."

He put the wheel over and a faint cheering reached them across the water. The three faces at the window vanished and by the time he had turned the barge head to tide and eased her alongside the end of the wharf, they had re-appeared by the railings at the top of the wharf steps.

"Take a turn round that end bollard until we know if we've got a freight," Punchy told Jem, "no sense in going in if we're wasting our time."

Jem did as he was told and the *Windhawk* swung in the tideway, straining a little to be on her way as the ebb quickened.

"Oh Jem, thank goodness you came in!" Nora leapt on board and almost threw her arms around him in relief. She poured out her story in such haste that Jem and Punchy gleaned little beyond the fact that some terrible crisis had occurred. But she was soon followed on board by Annie. Seeing her distress Jem overcame his natural reserve far enough to put his arm around her shoulder and, steering her to a seat on the hatch coaming, was soon made acquainted with the sorry tale of Lady Crumleigh's stolen ring.

"And now," she concluded, "poor Uncle Fred has gone off to tackle the thieves single-handed not to mention the danger to that lad and the little girl. Oh Jem, 'tis like a judgment on us for going against his wishes as my guardian and engaging ourselves wilfully when we had no right. Goodness knows what trouble we've bought on them as well as ourselves."

The sight of her tears made Jem feel so emotional that he was forced to swallow hard. He patted her hair tentatively once or twice and said thickly, "Never fear, my lass. 'T will all be right in the end. Dad and me 'll see to it."

"That's right," said Punchy. "We'll be away without even taking on a freight, and we'll catch that old fool Batey, begging your pardon my dear, I mean your Uncle Fred, before he makes the Medway."

In fact Punchy thought to himself that Batty Fred was in far greater danger from wind and weather than from jewel thieves. He seriously doubted whether the *Blackbird* could make the Medway in the rising wind with her spars intact, and was more concerned for Daniel and Rosie than for her mad old Skipper.

Annie turned up her tear-filled blue eyes to gaze at him gratefully. "Oh dear Mr Kitson, I knew I could rely on you, but you won't let my Jem come to any harm, will you? I must get back to the house now with the children before Mr Fanshaw returns from the Admiralty."

Punchy and Jem assured her yet again that everything should be done in safety and, raising their heads from the contemplation of her pretty tear-stained face, found to their consternation that the *Windhawk* was no longer moored to the end of the Lots Road wharf, but with a two-knot tide under her and a west-south-west wind catching her small bridge sail, was already well out into the tideway and bearing down upon Battersea Bridge.

Even as Punchy yelled, "Who the blazes untied that mooring rope!" he was at the wheel and bringing his barge under control. "Was that you, Charlie?" he demanded, seeing guilt writ large all over the young face in front of him.

"Yes," said Charlie with staggering honesty, since the truth was bound to come out anyway. "If I hadn't done you'd have put us ashore with Annie."

"Oh Master Charlie, now look what you've done!" Annie was all of a dither. "What will your father say if he finds us gone?"

"Nora left a note."

"You must put us ashore farther down, Mr Kitson. There's a little pier just beyond Battersea Bridge."

"It would waste time," protested Charlie.

"I shall do just as Annie says," said Punchy firmly, "this business may end in a scrap. 'Twill be no place for women and children."

Nora seethed inwardly and almost made up her mind to join the suffragette movement. Then she played her trump card. "Do you think Annie will be better off spending the night in prison, then?" she demanded. "Locked up with thieves and pickpockets and . . . "

" . . . and loose women?" added Charlie. He was not at all sure what loose women were but Cook often referred to them in tones of deepest disapproval.

"Don't interrupt, Charlie!" said Nora crossly.

"Oh, Miss Nora," protested Annie, "your Pa is a good man. He'll never let them put me in prison."

"Ah, but Lady Crumleigh might," said Charlie, "she might come round with some coppers to arrest you."

That settled it. There was no way Jem was going to

allow his Annie to be taken away to prison — especially one full of loose women — for stealing a ring he had given her as a pledge of his undying love. In spite of her pleas they passed on downstream until the familiar landmarks had all vanished astern and at last she abandoned her protests.

Charlie and Nora were in their element. Ever since they had first come to the house by the river they had dreamed of a barge that would carry them away down its busy stream. As Punchy steered the unmasted *Windhawk* skilfully through the busy river traffic, they gazed in wonder at famous bridges and buildings which took on a whole new magical dimension when seen from the river.

Below Tower Bridge even greater delights were in store. The great disadvantage of living above the bridges was that the passing barges were never seen in the full glory of their sails, and now as the *Windhawk* moored up to begin raising her gear Nora and Charlie went wild with excitement.

They knew the routine, for the mast and sprit had to be raised at the wharf before loading and unloading the holds, but this time the familiar tasks gave promise of the rare thrill to come. They scampered backwards and forwards, getting in Jem and Punchy's way in their efforts to be useful. But when Annie cautiously suggested that it might be quicker and safer if they stood by her and watched, Punchy winked at her good-naturedly and said to let them be as they were doing a grand job. It never ceased to amaze Annie, even after a lifetime spent in and around sailing barges, that two men or at times one man and a boy could raise unaided the many tons' weight of a sailing barge's massive spars. Yet so it was. One minute every inch of her decks aft of the mast case seemed cluttered up with a tangle of spars, sails and ropes and then, with the wire of the stayfall in place, the handles were put into the windlass in the bows and with a little puffing and straining the whole tangled mass began to rise. Moreover, as it rose it managed to sort itself out with very little trouble. With the exception of a stray rope caught up here and there and soon cleared by Charlie and Nora, every block and tackle seemed to know precisely where it belonged. With gathering speed the spars rose high above the decks and the *Windhawk*'s jumbled gear miraculously resolved itself into a mast, a mainsail, and the massive sprit. When these were secured, Charlie was allowed to haul up on the heelrope, raising the topmast to where Jem waited aloft to secure it with a metal fid.

And then came the marvel which the two children had only seen from the distance on an occasional steamer trip down the river: the sight of a Thames barge with all her sails curving; only this time it was their beloved *Windhawk* and they were not wistful onlookers, they were on board and playing out in reality their favourite dream.

The *Windhawk* lived up to her name. In her dark-russet plumage, she mastered the wind and rode in her own element like her namesake borne on the high summer air. Her elegance seemed effortless: her powerful strength masked by the sheer beauty of her form.

"We shall catch them up, shan't we?" said Nora to Punchy. "I mean that old crock *Blackbird* could never sail at this sort of speed."

Punchy grinned at her enthusiasm. "I wouldn't put anything past old Fred," he said, shaking his head. "Depends how far he towed down, and how hard he drives her. He may be an old fool but not with his hands at the wheel of a barge. He beat me home many a time in the old racing days. I reckon we shall either pass him with his masts snapped or find he's home before us."

When they were past Gravesend and through the Lower Hope into Sea Reach, the estuary widened and Charlie came aft to beg for the loan of Punchy's telescope.

"Well, you watch it don't go over the side," said Punchy cautiously. "What you want it for?"

"I want to keep a look out for that German submarine," Charlie explained, "that one that sank the *Bulldog*."

Punchy laughed. "You don't believe that old submarine tale do you?" he asked. "Why, it turned out to be just an accident while they was loading ammunition: it said so in the paper."

This time it was Charlie's turn to laugh. "That was written by our father," he said, and adding disrespectfully, "if you believe that, Punchy Kitson, you'll believe anything!" he went to take up his lookout post in the bows.

Thirteen

Daniel was woken suddenly by the sound of raised voices. It took him a few moments to work out why he was so cold and cramped, but as memory came back to him he was at once on his guard. The voices were coming from the direction of the rough-stuff pile. He inched his way towards a knot-hole in the old boat's timbers, the movement setting up waves of pins and needles in one leg so intense that he had to bite his lip to stay quiet. Through the knot-hole he could see three men standing in a huddle and talking noisily. Either they had no reason to suspect any eavesdropper or some excitement had overwhelmed their discretion. Daniel moved back to tell Batty Fred. "Mr Batey," he hissed, "Mr Batey, I think it's them . . ." But the only answer was a mumbled protest as the old man settled a little deeper into his dreams.

Daniel had no idea how long they had all been sleeping or how long ago the men had arrived. They might have been searching the pile for hours. If so, had they at last found the booty they were seeking? He strained his ears to hear what they were saying but they were too far away. Daniel considered the problem of waking up Batty Fred: if he shook the old man there was a chance that he might wake Rosie too, and she was at an age when she did not take kindly to being woken in the night. In her half-sleeping confusion, she would protest loudly and her cries would alert the men to their hiding place. There was nothing for it but to investigate by himself. Since his leg seemed to have regained its function, he crept silently across the intervening space until he reached the far side of the heap and could make out what the voices were saying. There seemed to be some kind of an argument going on and one voice was raised above the rest, " . . . and I tell you that if anything's missing from the bag, we're likely to be found face down on the foreshore tomorrow morning with a sack over our 'eads."

" 'Ow would he know that we nicked it? Some of it's goin' to be missin' anyway."

"That's right," the third voice supported the second, "I told you that fellow in the pub had a ring from it."

"A ring could have fell out through the 'ole in the bag, but if anything bigger is missin', 'e'll come down on us for it. Tie it up again and let's get away from 'ere."

A prickle of fear raised the hair on the back of Daniel's neck. His sense of triumph at having been right about the thieves was somewhat tarnished by the realization that he was dealing with violent and unscrupulous men. He had an uncomfortable mental picture of himself "face down on the foreshore with a sack over his head". Instinctively he drew back into the shadows to puzzle out his next move. Even if he had found the thieves, what was he to do about it? He was still a long way from catching them; indeed at that moment his main concern was to keep as still as possible for fear lest they should catch him.

Cautiously he peered out again. The men seemed to have agreed that discretion was the better part of greed, for the argument had died down and, as Daniel watched, the three men moved away along the pathway towards the brick field. He waited until he was absolutely certain that the were too far away to hear him and then went hurrying back to wake Batty Fred and Rosie.

"Mr Batey, Mr Batey! You must wake up."

Dragged reluctantly back into consciousness, Batty Fred's only thought was that his mouth was as dry as old cinders and tasted like a rough-stuff pile. He decided that he urgently needed to hurry down to the Anchor and Hope for a quick pint or two.

"Mr Batey, you can't! Don't you remember? We were lying in wait for the jewel thieves. We all fell asleep, Mr Batey, and they came and now they've gone and, oh, if you don't hurry up they'll get away."

" . . . well . . . I dunno about no jewel thieves . . . " Batty Fred mumbled sulkily to himself.

"But if we don't catch them, Annie will go to prison!"

Batty Fred woke up abruptly as the whole sordid muddle came back to him. Something about that dratted Jem Kitson getting his Annie into a mess with some stolen ring. Well, *he* would put it all right. Her old Uncle Fred would catch the thieves and clear her name, and she would be eternally grateful and would learn from this terrible experience always to do just as he told her in future, and never, never to have anything to do with those unspeakable Kitsons again!

He was on his feet as fast as his ageing joints would allow and, anger lending him strength, he swung the still sleeping Rosie up across his shoulder and said loudly, "Right, lad! Which way did they go?"

Daniel cringed at the reckless booming of his voice. "Mr Batey, please! We must be quiet or we shall end up with sacks over our heads and . . . oh, do come on they're heading back through the brickyard and there's three of them, so I don't know how we can tackle them but we mustn't let them out of our sight."

Daniel could just make out the three figures ahead of them along the path. He thought quickly: it couldn't be too late because lights were still visible in the windows of distant houses. These small clusters of cottages where the brickies and the muddies lived were built wherever a patch of firmer, drier ground rose above the waterlogged muddy wastes of the saltings. But to reach any of them in search of help was out of the question, for a hundred-and-one salty streams and inlets ran between them like a vast maze. To find in the darkness the firm cindered pathways that linked them would take time and meanwhile the three men would be gone. The only hope was that the men themselves might take a path that passed close by one of the rows of cottages. But if they did, he thought, they might well find only the womenfolk and children at home, with the strong-armed brickies all departed to the Anchor and Hope for their evening's drinking. If only the three men had gone the other way down to Dora's for a quick drink after their cold unappetizing search. It was really most unreasonable of them not to have done so, he thought indignantly: it would have been in character and would certainly have made his task easier. Once he had spread word of Annie's predicament among the muddies, the brickies, and the barge crews, the three rogues would have been dealt with swiftly and with relish . . .

As it was, all they could do was to keep the men in sight at all costs and hope something would turn up. He glanced up yet again to make sure that they were still there and found that the road through the brick field was empty.

Panic seized him.

"Mr Batey," he hissed urgently. "They've gone. Did you see which way they went?"

"Gone down towards the wharf," said Batty Fred. "Must 'ave got a boat down there."

Daniel's heart sank. Once they were gone out into the winding swatchways of the saltings, they would be impossible to find.

"We'll have to follow them in the dinghy," he said knowing as he said it that one old man and a boy could never keep up with strong men at the oars.

" 'opeless! Not a chance in the open water," said Batty Fred. "We'll 'ave to go after them in the *Blackbird*. They'll cross the water to the Isle of Grain like as not, or else why come by boat in the first place?"

"But they might go in among the creeks," suggested Daniel.

"And what if they do?" asked Batty Fred scornfully, "tide's rising fast, *Blackbird* don't draw more than three feet: and I knows them creeks like the back of my 'and."

Daniel began to have a reassuring feeling that the old man might after all prove an asset rather than a liability. It was true that no one, not even Punchy Kitson himself, knew his way about the Medway estuary better than Batty Fred.

As they reached the mud wharf, they could see the dinghy with the three men in it rowing its way along the rippled, moon-silvered pathway that ran down the water of the creek.

"Be careful," said Daniel. "They may see us."

"And what if they do? They don't know we're after them. I'm just a sailorman rowing back to my barge after a pint or two, to raise sail and get out before the flood quickens. Tide's slack, wind in my favour . . . why should they suspect anything?"

Once again Batty Fred had the better of him, and when he added, "I'll row lad, you keep an eye on them," Daniel did as he was told without argument.

Rosie slept on peacefully, sprawled across Daniel's lap, as they made their way down the creek towards the *Blackbird*. The wind had scoured a wide gap in the cloud and the full moon lit up the silvery waters as the tide turned silently and began once again its inexorable spread across the wide mudflats.

One of the men in the other boat stared at them suspiciously as they followed behind, but seemed to lose interest as they turned aside to board the *Blackbird*.

It took a matter of minutes only to slip the rope from the buoy and loosen the brails on the *Blackbird's* mainsail. Daniel hooked the main sheet block to the travelling iron ring of the main horse and then took the wheel while Batty Fred put his greater strength to hauling in the main sheet as the great sail filled with wind.

During this flurry of activity they lost sight of the dinghy, which had pulled steadily ahead, but once back at the wheel Batty Fred sent Daniel to set the foresail to keep a look out. Soon he spotted the tiny craft a hundred yards or so ahead of them. Powered by the wind the *Blackbird* was faster, but with the tide low she was forced to tack backwards and forwards in the narrow channel of deep water that ran down the centre of the creek, while the oarsmen set their course straight ahead. Even so the barge was gaining steadily and Daniel could see that once they were out of the creek into Kethole Reach, the barge would be able to sail rings around her quarry. Yet what good could they do, he thought, but follow and hope. The two of them did not have the strength to take their quarry by force.

And then, as they came out into open water, he saw in the moonlight a sight that made his heart leap. Sailing up river, rounding the bend from Saltpan, came a vision of beauty: a barge like a soaring bird. Forgetting discretion in his excitement and delight, Daniel turned to shout the good news back to Batty Fred.

"Oh, Mr Batey, we've got them now! They're trapped between us and the *Windhawk*."

But Batty Fred's response to this news was not at all what he expected. Half a lifetime of hostility towards the Kitsons was not to be abandoned lightly for the convenience of the moment. Indeed Batty Fred saw no possible advantage in the *Windhawk*'s intrusion into the pursuit. It was his aim to prove to Annie that he alone could save her from the peril into which Jem Kitson had so negligently placed her. The idea that that same villainous Jem Kitson and his unspeakable father should appear in the nick of time and play the heroes, stealing Batty Fred's glory and winning Annie's gratitude . . . ! The very idea was insufferable.

His loud bellow of fury was echoed by another from

Rosie, who had woken up to add to the confusion. Daniel had finished setting the foresail and ran to attend to his sister for fear that in her halfwaking state she would not realize that they were under sail.

"Be careful, Rosie!" He grabbed her as she was emerging from the fo'c'sle, where Batty Fred had settled her. "We may tack at any minute, you really ought to stay below!"

"Where are we?" Rosie rubbed the sleep out of her eyes with a small clenched fist, and as she did so Daniel caught a sudden gleam of red in the moonlight.

"Rosie?" he said. "What's that on your finger?"

Rosie's hand vanished into the pocket of her pinafore and emerged wearing nothing more than the dirt under the fingernails. "Nothing," she said quickly, waving it for him to see.

Daniel tried to remember when he had last seen the ring. Had Rosie ever returned it to Charlie? Or had it been forgotten in the confusion of Batty Fred's return . . .

"Rosie," he said sternly, "have you still got . . . ?" but his sentence was never completed.

As the *Blackbird* and the *Windhawk* rapidly closed the distance between them, Batty Fred did the first unseamanlike act of his whole career as a barge Skipper. It was as if a lifetime of bitterness and hostility had eaten away at his powers of judgment until under one more unexpected pressure, something finally snapped. Blind to everything except a fierce determination to prevent the Kitsons from intercepting his quarry, Batty Fred spun his wheel without warning, and gybed the *Blackbird* across the *Windhawk's* bows. It was an incredibly irresponsible thing to do and marked the full extent of Batty Fred's derangement.

The sudden change of direction threw the *Blackbird* into confusion. Rosie and Daniel, taken off-balance, disappeared down the fo'c'sle hatch again and landed in a confused heap at the bottom of the ladder. Rosie got the worst of it, being underneath. Still only half awake and with a rising bump on her head, she remained silent for a moment only because Daniel's weight had winded her. But once he clambered to his feet allowing her to take a breath, she set up a scream which sounded to Daniel as if she had at the very least broken a limb. Convinced that the *Blackbird* had been involved in a collision and might even now be letting water below deck, Daniel was torn between hurrying to give Batty Fred some assistance, and a feeling that he must get the injured Rosie up on deck in case it should be necessary to abandon ship.

The fact that the *Blackbird* had not been hit head on by the *Windhawk*, was due entirely to Punchy Kitson's skill. Approaching down Kethole Reach, he had seen the *Blackbird* ahead but on a course which would allow him to pass easily astern of her. In the moonlight he had registered with irritation the presence of a unlighted dinghy on his starboard bow, but had no way of knowing that it was the *Blackbird*'s quarry or that in passing close by it the *Windhawk* was in any way impeding the hunter. Nothing was further from his mind than any attempt to steal Batty Fred's thunder, so that when the old mud-barge gybed across his bows, he was taken completely by surprise. With a string of oaths that burned Nora's ears and left Charlie open-mouthed with admiration, Punchy Kitson put her wheel over and spun the *Windhawk* almost within her own length on to an avoiding tack, convinced with some reason that Batty Fred had finally gone round the bend. For a long moment the two barges continued to converge, but as the *Windhawk* recovered herself her bow sprit passed within feet of the *Blackbird*'s side. If Batty Fred had had a strong crewman to help him to bring the *Blackbird* under way again after the gybe, he might have escaped the consequences of his own foolhardiness. But with Daniel out of action, the old man lost valuable time in his single-handed struggle to bring the great mainsail under control. As the two barges passed alongside each other a sudden gust of wind carried the *Blackbird* against the *Windhawk*'s side, and with a juddering crack their great black leeboards locked together.

When Daniel, having assured himself that all Rosie's limbs were still in working order, emerged on to the deck, he was met by a scene of indescribable confusion. Both the *Blackbird* and the *Windhawk* were at a standstill under wildly flapping canvas, and while Jem Kitson was struggling with a boat-hook to prise the jammed leeboards apart, Batty Fred appeared to be on the point of attacking him with a similar weapon.

"You get that hook out of my barge, Jem Kitson!" he was bawling. "Or you'll get what's long been comin' to you. I'll teach you to get my Annie into trouble!"

"Mr Batey, please . . . he's only trying to help!" Daniel seized the handle of the boat-hook and tried to pull the old man away.

"Who needs his help? Us Bateys never needed no help from them Kitsons," and Batty Fred lunged at Jem, who ducked sideways and said,

"Git out of it, yer silly old fool!"

As Daniel was struggling with the old man, Charlie and Nora arrived to see what was happening and soon Rosie came clambering her way up from below so as not to miss the fun.

"What are you two doing on the *Windhawk*?" she demanded of Charlie and Nora. "And why are the boats stuck together?"

"That old maniac went straight across our bows," shouted Charlie above the noise of the wind and flapping canvas, and Daniel shouted back:

"We were after the jewel thieves: three of them in a dinghy . . . goodness knows where they are now."

"How do you know it was them? Had they got the loot?"

"Yes, but we'll never catch them after this . . . "

Punchy had left the wheel to add his strength to the task of separating the two craft. His arrival might well have brought a renewed assault from Batty Fred if he had not been distracted by the sight of his beloved Annie hovering excitedly in the background.

"Annie Batey! What are you doin' on there with them blamed Kitsons? You come over here on to the *Blackbird* at once, do you hear me!"

"Uncle Fred, do calm down! We came to help. You'll ruin everything with your temper tantrums."

"Temper tantrums! I'll thank you to keep a civil tongue in your head, Annie Batey!"

But at that moment the wind, which had been keeping the two barges against one another, slackened its hold long enough for Punchy to push them a little way apart. As he did so, there was a cracking sound and the *Blackbird's* leeboard was bent outwards as the rotten wood parted from its fixings.

Daniel had never before seen anyone who actually danced with rage as Batty Fred did now. But too many other things were happening at once. Charlie was waving the telescope furiously at him as the two barges began to drift apart again. Daniel heard him shout, "I can see them over there . . . " he gestured in the direction of the saltings, "four men . . . in a dinghy . . . running for cover . . . "

He must be wrong, thought Daniel, there were only three men; but the light was bad. It gave him something to take Batty Fred's mind off the indignity he had suffered at the hands of the Kitsons.

"Mr Batey! The jewel thieves are escaping . . . they're heading for the shelter of the saltings, you must take the wheel, Mr Batey, we're drifting down river."

He could see that Punchy now had the *Windhawk* well under control and was going in pursuit of the dinghy, which was clearly visible now in a patch of moonlight.

Batty Fred saw it too.

He swore picturesquely. "If that Paunchy Kitson thinks he can steal my thunder he's got another think comin'," he muttered ominously as he brought the *Blackbird* under the power of the wind again. "Carrying off respectable girls like my Annie . . . I'll show that villain." He made it sound as if the *Windhawk* was engaged in the white slave traffic.

Watching the barge ahead, Daniel saw that she had come to a halt. He heard the rattle as she dropped anchor at the edge of the tideway and saw her sails hastily brailed.

"I think they're going to follow in the *Windhawk*'s dinghy," he told Batty Fred. "There's not enough water in the swatchways to go in under sail."

"Not for them, there ain't," said Batty Fred with satisfaction, "but the *Blackbird*'ll make it; she don't draw so much; built for the canals she was."

Sizing up the inlet down which the dinghy had disappeared, Daniel had his doubts. "I don't think we could make it even so," he called back nervously, "it's too narrow."

Then he realized that Batty Fred had changed direction.

"Well, we ain't goin' in that way, young clever dick," he said nastily, "because Fred Batey knows these saltings better than any other man alive. That inlet will bring them out into the Saltfleet mud hole and we're goin' to catch them as they come out of it."

It seemed to Daniel that they were sailing directly away from their quarry, and although he reckoned that in any case Jem and Punchy had more chance of apprehending the thieves than he did with Batty Fred, he was reluctant to miss the excitement of the chase. But a few minutes later Batty Fred put the *Blackbird* about and headed straight for the dark shoreline.

Daniel and Rosie stood side by side in the bows watching the scrub-covered saltings growing closer, and the realization grew in them that the creek was not there.

"We are going to hit the land," said Rosie with interest. "Do you think Mr Batey has gone mad?"

As the *Blackbird* continued inexorably on her way, Daniel decided that he had. "Mr Batey, I think we're in the wrong place," he shouted. "We're going to go aground," but Batty Fred only shouted back derisively, "Go teach your grandmother to suck eggs, young Daniel Swann."

And then as the saltings loomed so close that Daniel could have thrown a stone into the undergrowth, Batty Fred shouted and the *Blackbird* tacked again. Miraculously a wide silver pathway, running almost parallel to the tideway, opened up ahead of them and the *Blackbird* moved smoothly round into the hidden creek.

Rosie clapped her hands with delight at this unexpected trick, and Daniel was overcome with admiration. "How did you know it was there, Mr Batey?" he called. "I mean without lights or markings . . . ?"

The respect in his voice was balm to Batty Fred's wounded ego. " 'Cos I've been in and out of it more times than you've 'ad hot dinners, that's how," said the old man smugly, "leads to a big old mud hole used to take six mud barges at a time in the old days. One of the widest and deepest mud holes on the saltings. And that's the way them thieves'll come in the dinghy and when they do they'll find us ready and waiting to meet 'em."

They rounded the gentle curve of the creek and Rosie pointed and shouted, "There they are!"

There was indeed a dinghy ahead of them, but it seemed to be moving away from them.

"It's going the wrong way," said Daniel.

"Well, they seen our sails coming round the bend, so they turned and ran," said Batty Fred confidently.

"But there are four men in it," added Daniel frowning thoughtfully. Charlie had said that he had seen a dinghy with four men in it. Daniel began to have an uneasy feeling that there was more than one dinghy around roaming the swatchways in the darkness without lights. Perhaps they were even following the wrong one.

As if to confirm his suspicions, the curving creek

179

widened suddenly on the starboard side into a wide sheet of hidden water, and there on the far side of it were two more dinghies rowing across the abandoned mud hole.

Rosie clapped her hands. "Now there are three of them!" she said delightedly.

But before Daniel could sort out which was which, he noticed something else: an unfamiliar object like a small tower which projected above the water in the centre of the mud hole. Batty Fred did not seem to have noticed it. He was too busy staring at the three dinghies ahead in an effort to decide which was the hated Kitsons and which one was his own lawful prey.

Daniel stared at the tower-like object with an uneasy feeling that he had seen something like it before . . . It was too large to be a buoy, though distance could be deceptive in the moonlight. He narrowed his eyes and moved his head slightly from side to side in an effort to resolve the uncertain image in his mind . . . There were two tube-like objects projecting above the tower and what seemed to be a number on the side. Then as they came almost abreast of it and the changing angle made the shape of it clearer, he knew with a sudden awful certainty what it was . . . and even as he began to shout, he knew that he would be too late.

"Mr Batey! Mr Batey! It's the submarine! It's dead ahead . . . under the water. Go about, Mr Batey, before we hit her . . ."

Even as he yelled and made one wild hopeless grab at the wheel, he was thrown off-balance. The *Blackbird* reared up out of the water as her shallow bows ran on to the submerged foredeck of the submarine. The invisible gun mounted there tore a wide hole in her rotten planking, tilting her sideways and her mast stays, already weakened by the collision with the *Windhawk*, parted under the strain. Her massive sprit fell sideways carrying the vast mainsail with it, and her mast snapped like a matchstick under the weight of them. Daniel had only a moment in which he saw the impending disaster against the moonlit brightness of the sky. He grabbed at Rosie, threw her to the deck and spread out his arms to shield her. Then all became dark and silent.

Fourteen

There was water across his face and a strange buzzing in his ears. Struggling back to consciousness, Daniel wondered whether he was drowning and waited for his whole life to flash before his eyes as more than one sailorman had assured him it would do in the circumstances.

He conjured up the face of Punchy Kitson, oddly lit by lamplight, and then the face of Rosie . . . but as he tried to focus them more clearly his eyes were covered with water again and the images disappeared. He heard Punchy's voice saying, "Steady on Rosie, you'll drown the poor lad," and then, "look, now he's coming round, I told you he'd be all right, my love."

Daniel tried to open his eyes again but his head ached and it was less effort simply to lie still and try to remember what had happened.

He could hear Rosie anxious and tearful, "Ma looked like that," she was saying, "and they took her away in a nambulance. You won't let them take Danny away in a nambulance will you, Mr Kitson?"

"They'd 'ave a job, love," Punchy sounded reassuringly cheerful, "We're stuck on top of a submarine in the middle of the mud hole . . . "

At these words the most recent events in Daniel's life flashed before his eyes with startling clarity but not, he decided, because he was drowning. He opened his eyes and tried to sit up.

"Are you all right, Rosie?" he asked rather unnecessarily.

Finding she was not after all in danger of losing him, Rosie remembered her own grievances.

"You fell on top of me," she said reproachfully and remembering their earlier fall down the fo'c'sle ladder she added, "you did it again."

"Sorry," said Daniel. "I don't remember much about it."

"Once more," said Rosie ominously, "and you're a dead duck!"

Daniel's head was clearing rapidly. "What happened to Batty Fred?" he asked. "And how did you get here, Punchy?"

"Well, we rowed across as soon as we saw you'd hit something. My word," he shook his head admiringly, "that was quite a way to go if you're going to wreck a boat. Old Fred don't do nothing by halves!"

"He isn't dead, is he?" said Daniel anxiously, realizing with surprise that he really cared about the disagreeable old man.

"Old Fred? Take more than a Hun submarine to do 'im in. Listen!"

Daniel listened and became aware of the muffled but insistent sound of cursing. "Where is he?"

"Trapped under his own mainsail, silly old fool," Punchy laughed. "Jem and the two kids is trying to cut a hole and get 'im out but he keeps yelling, 'Leave my sail alone, you vandals.' As if it was any good to him now! I reckon Jem should leave 'im there to stew in his own juice."

"What happened to the jewel thieves?" asked Daniel as the memories crowded back, "And the men in the other dinghy . . . and what about the submarine, the Huns will all come out and capture us and . . . "

"Steady on, old lad." Punchy's voice was soothing. "One thing at a time. First of all no one is coming out of that submarine because *Blackbird* is sitting firmly on top of the escape hatch with her sprit lodged across its conning tower. So any old Huns inside will stay put until the powers-that-be comes to deal with them. That is all except the four what was in the dinghy. On their way back after a bit of sabotage, I reckon. Well, they've gone off into the swatchways and them jewel thieves too. Serve 'em all right if they meets up with each other. Them Huns is armed, you know; one of them took a pot shot at us as they scarpered into the darkness."

"We ought to get after them," said Daniel, "the thieves, I mean. It's the only way we can prove that Annie is innocent."

"All in good time, young Daniel. They're as safe as houses in there. Two square miles of saltings with more twists and turns and dead ends than that there 'Ampton Court Maze what they boasts about. I reckon we can safely leave 'em in there to cool their heels for a bit. So if you can stand, lad, we'll go and help Jem to get that old fool Batey out of the mess he's landed 'imself in."

Batty Fred had been lucky to escape the falling spars but with the heavy mast landing on one side of him and the massive sprit on the other, he had been flattened on the deck by the great spread of canvas. Seeing his predicament Daniel had to admit that Jem's solution of cutting a hole in the mainsail with his knife, was Fred's only possible way out.

Batty Fred saw it differently. Unaware as yet of the extent of the *Blackbird*'s disaster, he knew only that his arch-enemy Jem Kitson was carving a hole in his mainsail, and with one scrawny fist projecting through the hole, he was doing his best to impede his efforts. Nora had told him several times in her most authoritative tone "not to be so stupid," and Charlie had pointed out truthfully, if somewhat tactlessly, that the *Blackbird*'s mainsail was "a mass of patched holes, anyway". However, their well-meant intervention only seemed to enrage the old man more, while Annie's gentle plea to "calm down a little Uncle Fred, and let Jem rescue you," produced only strangled cries of rage. Even Joxer was adding to the general confusion by barking and scrabbling at the sail cloth.

"Let me talk to him," said Daniel, taking the knife from Jem. He knelt beside the heaving canvas and racked his brains for some acceptable way of telling Batty Fred the worst. Then he had an inspiration.

"Mr Batey, it's me, Daniel Swann," he began. "Do keep still while I try to get you out."

The fist clenched and shook itself at him and the muffled voice shouted, "You leave my mainsail alone, you little varmint, you think I ain't got damage enough with my spars gorn, without I 'as to buy a new mainsail?"

"But Mr Batey, didn't you know? You've captured that Hun submarine, single-handed . . . you'll be a hero, Mr Batey . . . "

The heaving mass under the canvas went quite still and Batty Fred's astonished voice said, "I did?" and then, "I will? . . . an 'ero you say?"

Daniel began quietly cutting a flap in the canvas. "Of course, Mr Batey," he said soothingly. "The way you deliberately ran the *Blackbird* up on that submarine so that it couldn't escape was real splendid. Dora will be so proud of you. Why I shouldn't be at all surprised if the King don't give you a medal."

"The King? . . . A medal?" said the stunned voice from beneath the sail.

Daniel had almost finished his task. "Yes," he said. "Of course, the *Blackbird*'s a wreck, Mr Batey, but she went serving her King and Country, and there's bound to be a lot of compensation money."

He folded back the flap of canvas and Batty Fred's head emerged, the small, beady, red eyes gleaming greedily.

"Did you say compensation money, lad?" he asked. "A hero . . . a medal . . . *and* compensation money?" Already his mind was working on the new image. He saw himself at the bar of the Anchor, the medal gleaming on his chest, the money jingling in his pocket, and Dora repeating yet again to her admiring customers the story of his heroic exploit.

He squeezed his way out through the hole so wrapped in thought that he did not even notice that it was Punchy Kitson's strong hand that helped him to his feet. Not until

Punchy said with a laugh, "Git on, you old fraud, you never even knew that Hun was there!"

Batty Fred turned to him in fury. "I did so, Paunchy Kitson! What do you know about it? Just 'cos you Kitsons ain't got the guts to give your all for King and Country . . . "

"Come on, you can save all that for Dora," said Punchy. "I'm going off after them thieves."

Batty Fred hesitated. Even with the thought of the glory that was already due to him, he was reluctant to let the Kitsons be heroes in Annie's eyes. It would only encourage this unthinkable idea she had got into her head about marrying Jem. But the desire to shine before Annie warred with the equally pressing desire to take himself off to the Anchor and play the hero before Dora. He stared gloomily across the forbidding darkened wastes of the saltings.

"You could row around there all night and never find 'em," he said. "Best to wait till daylight. Reckon they'll never find their way out anyway."

"Oh, they'll find their way out in time," said Punchy. "They'll gradually work their way in towards the shoreline and head for the only bit of light that's still shining at this time of night. With acres of mud everwhere else, they can only get ashore if they reach the Old Ferry Hard. Then they'll follow the causeway up towards the light and we all know where that will bring them out."

Daniel certainly knew and he laughed. "Of course," he said, "they'll come up the road past the Anchor and Hope."

"They will, indeed, lad! And long before they gets there, we shall have rowed across to the spit, walked up the beach, and we shall be ready and waiting for them. Why, they'll never know what hit them."

"But there are at least seven grown men, and some of them are armed," Daniel was more cautious. He had Rosie to think of and was not simple enough to imagine that he would be able to keep her out of the fight.

Punchy was climbing back into the dinghy. "We'll get help at the Anchor," he called.

"The customers will all have gone home."

"Don't you believe it, lad. The lights are still on. I reckon that means the muddies are having a day orf."

Jem and Annie, Nora and Charlie were already in the *Windhawk*'s dinghy.

"Are you coming with us, then, or are you going to stay with that old idiot?" called Charlie.

But Batty Fred, finding that Punchy was heading for the Anchor, was already manhandling the *Blackbird*'s tender over the side into the water.

"I'll go with Mr Batey," said Daniel. "After all, he is my Skipper."

As the other boat pulled away, he looked around him sadly at the broken *Blackbird* and the wreckage of his sailing career. Then he sighed. "Come on, Rosie," he said. "We'd better lend a hand."

The muddies' "day orf", to which Punchy had referred, was a custom as ancient as it was disreputable.

The road which the muddies took each day from the row of tiny cottages where they lived to the mud hole on the Lower Saltings passed at about its half-way point the rough track that led to the Anchor and Hope and the Old Ferry Hard. Invariably as the cheerful gang passed the junction of the two ways, some wag would suggest a diversion in the direction of Dora's bar, but ninety-nine times out of a hundred, in spite of a general murmur of approval, they continued on their appointed way to the mud hole. However, every now and then, for no particular reason beyond the fact that the fancy took him, the ganger would hang his jacket and his food bundle on the fence and say, "Right lads! Let's toss for it." Then he would take a brick from the small overgrown pile which had lain at the corner for as long as anyone could remember, and throw it high in the air. If it came down frog upwards there would be a loud cheer and hanging their belongings alongside the ganger's as the official sign of their independence, the muddies would depart *en masse* for a day off at the Anchor and Hope. There they would pass the time drinking, eating, talking, gambling and generally making merry.

Their wives, passing the junction on their way to do shopping, would "tut-tut" at the sight of their bundles on the fenceposts and observe to one another, "They're gorn orf, then?"

And as they came back an hour or so later they would comment with a sigh of resignation, "They're still gorn, then," and knew that there would be no need to prepare a meal that evening.

For the muddies' day off continued right through until the following day. Usually in the evening fights would break out, but they rarely got out of hand and at last in the early hours of the morning they would sing themselves to sleep by the fire in the bar and snore through the rest of the night face down in the spilt ale on Dora's tables. In the morning they would wake as cheerful as ever and after a quick hair of the dog would depart up the track to gather up their coats and their food tins from the fence and go on their way to the mud hole as if the intervening day had never been.

On the night of the "Great Fight with the Huns" — as it later became known in local legend — they had reached the sentimental stage of drunkenness and were singing a rousing if not over-tuneful chorus of a new popular song called "It's a Long Way to Tipperary," when the door was flung wide open and young Daniel Swann appeared breathless and panting in the doorway.

Dora was dozing elegantly with one delicate swan-like arm resting on the bar, her chin supported on her small white, bejewelled hand.

"Why, Daniel Swann," she said, blinking at him sleepily. "What are you doing 'ere at this time of the night . . . and that's never your little sister Rosie I see behind you, is it?"

"Oh Dora, please come and help. There's the most awful fight going on outside . . . "

At these words the muddies, who had broken off their song at the sound of the interruption, rose to their feet cheering and hurried outside, still clutching their ale mugs, to watch the fun.

From which you might suppose that the Huns, or at the very least the jewel thieves, had already put in an appearance. But you would be wrong. The fight which was under way was in fact between Punchy and Batty Fred and had started when they had jostled each other on the path up to the door, in their eagerness to be first to bring the news of the night's events to Dora.

As Punchy was by far the fitter and heavier of the two, having years of Dora's good cooking under his belt, he could easily have put an end to the fight with one powerful blow. But the long years with Dora had also made him contented and good-natured and he kept Batty Fred at arms' length as harmlessly as he could, rather like a wise old bull fending off a fierce bull terrier.

If Daniel hoped that the muddies would separate the two combatants he was disappointed. They gathered around in a laughing circle and egged on both men with good-natured cries of encouragement and Dora, to whom fights between her customers were an everyday occurrence, came out to see fair play. Charlie and Nora were delighted: they had led sheltered lives and had never before had the opportunity to watch uninterrupted while two grown men hammered each other. Rosie also seemed to find the spectacle enchanting, clapping her hands and jumping up and down until the ring leapt unnoticed from the pocket of her pinafore and fell into the shadows, down among the stony pebbles by the door of the inn.

In the general hubbub Daniel found it impossible to get anyone to listen to his story of the night's events, and his attempt to warn them of the impending arrival of the Huns and the jewel thieves fell upon already deafened ears. But, as things turned out, it didn't really matter. By the time the latter villains — exhausted and foul-tempered after their long, cold, nightmare journey through the maze of the saltings — came stumbling up the Old Ferry Hard, the muddies had got themselves into such a fighting mood that they were on the point of hitting each other, for want of any more acceptable opponents. One word from Daniel to draw their attention to the newcomers, and with cries of delight they waded straight into them, without even bothering to find out who they were or what unsavoury business brought them to that lonely corner of the world in the early hours of the morning.

The Huns arrived a little later. They were desperate men and finding that they had no other means of escape but to pass through the fighting throng which spilled out across the causeway, they attempted to do so by force of arms. Unfortunately for them, their cries of "Put up your hands!" delivered in a heavy and unintelligible German accent, passed unnoticed in the noise and confusion and they soon found themselves gathered into the mêlée. For the muddies were fair-minded men who liked an even fight and there were not enough jewel thieves to go round. There was one brief moment of danger when one of the more intrepid of the enemy submariners escaped to the edge of the throng and, drawing his gun, took aim at Punchy Kitson. But even as Daniel cried out an unheard warning, Dora, who never allowed such unsporting behaviour among her clientèle, felled him from behind with her pewter ale mug.

It was, as everyone agreed afterwards, unquestionably the best fight the Anchor and Hope had ever seen. As time went on, so many of the combatants landed in the rich mud beside the causeway only to struggle back, sticky and unrecognizable, into the fight that it eventually became impossible for anyone to tell friend from foe. But they all went on fighting anyway. When it was all over and the thirsty and exhausted victors decided to call it a day in favour of another round of ale, they wiped the clinging grey mud from their faces to reveal the broad smiles of Punchy, Jem and the muddies. But their survival was due entirely to superior muscle power or, in the case of the latter, a lifetime's experience of working in slippery mud.

And when on Dora's instructions the children took on the
enjoyable task of throwing buckets of water over the
recumbent bodies of the vanquished, it came as no
surprise to anyone when their efforts revealed the
disgruntled faces of the three jewel thieves, four Huns . . .
and Batty Fred.

Fifteen

But that was not quite the end of the story. The victors had barely completed the task of trussing up the vanquished, with the honourable exception of Batty Fred, who was carried mud and all into Dora's bar to be revived with brandy administered by her own fair hands, when Alfred Fanshaw arrived on the scene.

He had returned home to find his house in chaos, his wife groaning in a darkened room, his Cook locked in her bedroom and refusing to speak to anyone, his old nanny snoring drunkenly in the nursery, his port decanter empty, his housemaid gone out and his nursery maid and his two children missing. The only clue that offered any explanation of the monumental disaster that appeared to have struck at the roots of his family life, during his absence at the Admiralty, was a garbled note from Nora. This seemed to indicate that jewel thieves had broken in and had carried off the members of the Ladies' Luncheon Guild, while a scribbled postscript in Charlie's illegible handwriting appeared to add that he and Nora and Annie had been carried off on a boat called the *Windhawk* by a shady character named Punchy Kitson. Attempts to make sense of these notes by questioning Cook only produced an alternative theory, which was that the abduction of the Ladies' Guild had in fact been accomplished by German submariners, and an approach to Beatrice convinced him that Annie was almost certainly in league with a gang of ruthless jewel thieves led no doubt by the unscrupulous Punchy Kitson. Beatrice did also murmur something about a mouse, but Alfred put this down to her confused state of mind.

His most urgent problem was the pursuit and recovery of his children. For though in their noisier moments he had often wished them out of the way, he had not envisaged a solution as sudden and drastic as this present emergency.

The local police force were summoned and they in their turn contacted the Thames River Police, a splendid body of men whose records of the river traffic soon identified the *Windhawk* as a sailing barge skippered by one Samuel Kitson, an old experienced sailorman with an apparently unimpeachable record.

"Then why has he kidnapped my children, not to mention my nursery maid?" demanded Alfred Fanshaw testily, when acquainted with this fact.

"That remains to be seen," observed the Police Sergeant, cautious not to commit himself in view of the highly improbable nature of the story he had been called upon to investigate. Moreover he had a growing suspicion that Alfred Fanshaw might prove to be a dangerous lunatic.

It was established that the *Windhawk* belonged to the Lower Field Brick Company and that she had passed through Tower Bridge on her way down river only an hour or two earlier. Alfred Fanshaw demanded that the River Police should set out in pursuit, and by exaggerating the importance of his own position at the Admiralty, and hinting at a possible connection between Punchy Kitson and a German submarine, he persuaded them to place the services of a police launch at his disposal.

Proceeding down river with the last of the ebb, and with the advantages of steam power to overcome the adverse current when the tide turned, they reached the mouth of the Medway at about the time when the great fight began.

Alfred Fanshaw suspected that the *Windhawk* was carrying his children off into the clutches of some foreign power, but the crew of the police launch insisted on making the run up the Medway just to satisfy themselves that the *Windhawk* was not after all securely moored up at her own berth at the Lower Field. And just a mile or two short of her home creek they found her, anchored offshore at the edge of the tideway and as deserted as the famed *Marie Celeste*.

Alfred Fanshaw was beside himself, convinced that, like the crew of that notorious vessel, his children and their kidnappers would never be seen again. In search of information they set out again towards the only light discernible in the empty blackness of the saltings, a light which proved on closer examination to be coming from a small public house on the near-by headland. Sounds of singing, of laughter and loud talkative voices reached them as they approached, all strangely inappropriate for a den of thieves and kidnappers and yet . . .

"There they are!" cried Alfred Fanshaw triumphantly, catching sight of a tall girl with flying red hair who leapt and pranced in the light of the open doorway.

"Father!" cried Nora in dismay, not at all pleased at the prospect of having the best adventure of her whole life brought prematurely to an end.

There was a great deal of explaining to be done. The River Police found to their astonishment that Alfred Fanshaw had been right, not only in his improbable tale of jewel thieves, but also in his even more incredible assertion that enemy agents had a hand in the affair. They stopped treating him as a probable candidate for the local lunatic asylum, and allowed him to take charge in his official capacity as Admiralty spokesman. They found that he was quite content to allow them the full credit for the apprehension of the thieves and the recovery of the stolen jewellery — the sack and its contents having been retrieved from the mud by Daniel when the gang were laid low — but that a veil of secrecy was to be instantly drawn over the entire incident of the German submarine.

He explained with some eloquence to the assembled company the dire consequences that would ensue if it should ever be known that the Hun had penetrated so close to England's capital city. There would, he told them, be panic in the streets, alarm and despondency throughout the land, the country's war effort would be seriously undermined, and their beloved wives and children would never again sleep easily in their beds.

The fearsome picture he painted and his stirring appeal for their co-operation in hushing up the whole affair, swayed the hearts of his good-hearted and simple-minded listeners.

But Nora and Charlie were not deceived.

"Father is just afraid that his life will be unbearable if Cook and Lily Tompkins find out that they were right," hissed Charlie to Nora. As Nora, who was a fast thinker and not above a little blackmail, hissed back, "If he wants *us* to keep quiet, he will have to promise not to send us away to school . . . "

" . . . and to let us go sailing with Jem and Punchy," added Charlie gleefully.

Batty Fred, nursing a grudge and a painful jaw, was also sceptical.

"That's all very well," he protested suspiciously, "but if I ain't captured no submarine, which I 'ave, wot about my medal and my compensation money? I sacrificed my barge to stop them Huns from making a run for it . . . a racing barge my *Blackbird* was, and in first-class condition . . . gorn to a watery grave in defence of her King and Country."

"All that will be taken care of, I can assure you," said Alfred hastily, seeing the nasty gleam in Batty Fred's eyes. "The, er, medal may have to wait until the war is over, of course, but the compensation money will certainly be generous, provided that we can rely upon your co-operation."

Dora, who had visions of her bar being occupied all night by the discussions that would follow in the aftermath of the day's events, yawned elegantly and said firmly, "I think you can definitely tell His Majesty that he can rely on the discretion of everyone here, provided of course that Mr Batey is generously compensated, him being one of us and having lost his livelihood, as it were."

There was a general murmur of approval, for although

Batty Fred was nobody's favourite, he was, as Dora said, "one of them" and the people who lived and worked along the river had a strong sense of brotherhood.

"You have my assurance on that subject!" said Alfred pompously, for whatever his personal reasons for wanting to conceal the existence of a German submarine, he had no doubt that his superiors at the Admiralty would be equally anxious to prevent the embarrassing truth from leaking out.

"And," continued Dora, as if he had not interrupted, "and provided also that young Daniel Swann gets the reward for recovering the stolen jewels."

"What about me?" put in Batty Fred. "I was after them thieving varmints too!"

Dora frowned at him. "Now you're just being greedy, Fred," she admonished him, "and in any case it was Daniel that saved them from sinking into the mud . . . another few seconds and that sack would have been lost for ever!" She turned back inquiringly to Alfred Fanshaw, who assured her hastily that, "The Police Sergeant here will take note of all the particulars so that the young lad can be sure of his just reward."

"Well, that seems to be that, then," said Dora "and I think I might just allow one more round to keep out the cold night air, before I call 'Time, gentlemen, please'."

When the last drinks had been swallowed and the last particulars noted down, Nora and Charlie returned to Chelsea in the police launch with Alfred and the seven assorted prisoners, who were rapidly setting hard as their mud coating dried.

The muddies went to sleep in the bar along with Punchy, Jem and Batty Fred, but Dora took Daniel and

Rosie upstairs and, cleaning them up as best she could, put them to sleep in a large feather bed as soft as a cloud.

Early next morning, while the sleepers in the bar were still snoring, she roused the two children, fed and tidied them, and putting her fat little pony between the shafts of the pub's small dray cart, set off inland to find the hospital and reassure "poor Mrs Swann" that her children were both safe and sound.

The matron frowned and said it was not yet visiting hours and she did not know what things were coming to if people imagined that they could turn up at hospitals at any old time . . . and it wasn't as if Mrs Swann hadn't already got one visitor.

Daniel was so relieved to find that his mother was still alive, he would willingly have waited for hours for the chance to see her and it did not occur to him to ask who the other visitor was. But Dora was anxious to get back to her bar by lunchtime and, exerting all her considerable charm, she talked her way through the opposition.

Approaching down the long, echoing, ward between rows of identical iron bedsteds, Daniel felt his heart began to race as he saw the khaki figure that sat beside the end bed, screening the occupant from his eyes. If his boots had not clattered so noisily on the hard floor, he would have broken into a run. Rosie however had no such inhibitions: she gave a sudden cry of recognition and her small flying figure sped down the aisle and threw itself headlong into her father's arms.

They were not allowed to stay very long, only until they had proved to their mother that they were both alive and well, and had satisfied themselves that she was on the mend. Then Dora, promising the use of her cart so that they might return as often as visiting hours would permit, carried them all off home.

As they jogged peacefully along the country lanes, Daniel's father explained how he had been given "compassionate leave" to return home because of his wife's illness and the unexplained disappearance of his daughter.

Daniel felt terrible when he understood how much worry and concern he had caused by spiriting his sister away without a word. But Rosie told her father how she had been threatened with the orphanage and how bravely Daniel had rescued her, and Dora explained about the pursuit of the jewel thieves and — after first swearing him to secrecy — the capture of the Huns. Jack Swann listened intently and when the long saga ended, he put one hand on Daniel's shoulder and said, "You done the right thing, son. I'm real proud of you."

For Daniel it was the best moment of all.

Everything worked out very well. Batty Fred got his compensation money, but decided that he was too old now to start again with a new barge. So Dora took him aside and did a deal with him. It was agreed that, in return for giving his consent to Annie's marriage to Jem, Batty Fred would be allowed to take up residence at the Anchor and Hope as a paying guest. This would give him all the advantages of a home and hearthside, Dora's cooking, and the uncontestable right to his place at the end of the bar. Moreover, she pointed out, the match between his niece and her son — she conveniently overlooked Punchy's part in the affair — would unite them in one family and in due time, God willing, would give them both a share in the next generation. It was an offer which Batty Fred found he could not refuse.

Punchy on the other hand was horrified.

"You've invited that surly old fool to come and live with us?" he roared incredulously when Dora broke the news to him.

"As a paying guest, dear," said Dora calmly, "after all this is a public house, and it's not an unusual arrangement."

"We've never had paying guests before!"

"No one ever wanted to stay here before," said Dora truthfully.

"But he'll be following you around all day, making eyes at you, when I'm away on the *Windhawk*!" The picture of Batty Fred ogling Dora was unbearable.

"I'm sure I shall manage everything very well, dear." Dora was soothing but adamant. "It will be very useful to have a man to help about the place, lifting heavy barrels and such like."

This last observation was too much. If there was to be a man "helping about the place" it certainly was not going to be Batty Fred. Punchy Kitson frowned, thought hard, and came to a decision.

"That old fool Batey couldn't lift much more'n a pint tankard," he said. "I shall have to retire myself."

Dora beamed with delight. "Oh, that will be nice!" she said. "And then Jem can take over the *Windhawk*, with Daniel Swann to crew for him. Joxer can be their barge dog and Annie can live on board and look after them all."

She had it off so pat, and said it with such satisfaction, that Punchy began to wonder if she had planned it that way all along . . . which indeed she had. For Dora was no fool and she had easily foreseen that by taking Batty Fred as a paying guest, she could kill two birds with one stone.

It all turned out just as she had planned.

Everyone came to the wedding, which was the most splendid event the Lower Field had ever known.

The *Windhawk* was moored offshore and dressed with flags over all. The Anchor and Hope was decked out with flowers and white ribbons and Mr Jarvis kept his boys busy the whole of the previous day spraying the rough-stuff with Flit to keep the flies at bay.

Alfred Fanshaw came in a semi-official capacity, bringing Nora and Charlie, who were determined not to miss the fun — Beatrice being tactfully left behind because of the rigours of the journey. He made an excellent speech which was well received, especially his tribute to "this sturdy son of a maritime nation" and to "this charming flower of English maidenhood who will be sadly missed in my own household".

Rosie, cast as a bridesmaid in pink organdie, was in her element. Daniel stood watching her with his father and mother, while the photographer peered from beneath his black cloth and tried to arrange the giggling bridal party as elegantly as possible in front of the Anchor's lopsided doorway. As he spaced them out a little, placing Dora more prominently in her smart new gown, Daniel caught sight of a sudden red flash upon her finger. He craned his head a little to see the new ring more clearly. It was not the plain simple setting he remembered, but there was something very familiar about the fiery red stone in the centre. He glanced up at Dora's face and caught her eye upon him. She smiled, waved her hand so that he could get a better view and winked at him. Daniel laughed out loud and winked back. He had no idea how the ring had ended up on Dora's finger, but at least she could be relied upon to keep it out of mischief.

Anything or anyone, he thought: the ring, Batty Fred . . . or even his own future: all could be safely left in Dora's hands.